P9-DDH-672

Grease

Book, Music and Lyrics by
Jim Jacobs & Warren Casey

SAMUEL FRENCH

ISBN 978-0-573-68099-1

www.concordtheatricals.com
www.concordtheatricals.co.uk

MUSIC AND THIRD-PARTY MATERIALS USE NOTE

Licensees are solely responsible for obtaining formal written permission from copyright owners to use copyrighted music and/or other copyrighted third-party materials (e.g., artworks, logos) in the performance of this play and are strongly cautioned to do so. If no such permission is obtained by the licensee, then the licensee must use only original music and materials that the licensee owns and controls. Licensees are solely responsible and liable for clearances of all third-party copyrighted materials, including without limitation music, and shall indemnify the copyright owners of the play(s) and their licensing agent, Concord Theatricals Corp., against any costs, expenses, losses and liabilities arising from the use of such copyrighted third-party materials by licensees. For music, please contact the appropriate music licensing authority in your territory for the rights to any incidental music.

IMPORTANT BILLING AND CREDIT REQUIREMENTS

If you have obtained performance rights to this title, please refer to your licensing agreement for important billing and credit requirements.

GREASE, with book, music, and lyrics by Jim Jacobs and Warren Casey, presented by Kenneth Waissman and Maxine Fox in association with Anthony D'Amato, musical supervision and orchestrations by Michael Leonard, musical direction, vocal and dance arrangements by Louis St. Louis, by Douglas W. Schmidt, costumes by Carrie F. Robbins, lighting by Karl Eigsti, sound by Jack Shearing, production stage manager Joe Calvan, musical numbers and dances staged by Patricia Birch, directed by Tom Moore had its premiere performance February 14, 1972 at the Eden Theatre, N.Y.C. with the following cast:

CAST

(In Order of Appearance:)

MISS LYNCH	Dorothy Leon
PATTY SIMCOX	Ilene Kristen
EUGENE FLORCZYK	Tom Harris
JAN	Garn Stephens
MARTY	Katie Hanley
BETTY RIZZO	Adrienne Barbeau
DOODY	James Canning
ROGER	Walter Bobbie
KENICKIE	Timothy Meyers
SONNY LATIERRI	Jim Borrelli
FRENCHY	Marya Small
SANDY DUMBROWSKI	Carole Demas
DANNY ZUKO	Barry Bostwick
VINCE FONTAINE	Don BiUett
JOHNNY CASINO	Alan Paid
CHA-CHA DIGREGORIO	Kathi Moss
TEEN ANGEL	Alan Paul

MUSICAL NUMBERS

ACT ONE

Scene One: REUNION

"Alma Mater"......................*Miss Lynch, Patty and Eugene*

"'Alma Mater' Parody" .... *Pink Ladies, Burger Palace Boys*

Scene Two: CAFETERIA

"Summer Nights"................. *Sandy and Danny, Pink Ladies, Burger Palace Boys*

Scene Three: LOCKER ROOM

"Those Magic Changes" ....*Doody, Burger Palace Boys and Pink Ladies*

Scene Four: PAJAMA PARTY

"Freddy, My Love"...................... *Marty and Pink Ladies*

Scene Five: STREET CORNER

"Greased Lightnin'" .... *Kenickie and Burger Palace Boys*

Scene Six: SCHOOLYARD

"Rydell Fight Song"............................*Roger and Jan*

Scene Seven: PARK

"Mooning" ....*Roger and Jan*

"Look at Me, I'm Sandra Dee"...........................*Rizzo*

"We Go Together"............ *Pink Ladies and Burger Palace Boys*

ACT TWO

Scene One: ONSTAGE

"Shakin' at the High School Hop"................*Entire Company*

"It's Raining on Prom Night"........................... *Sandy*

"'Shakin' at the High School Hop' Reprise".......*Entire Company*

"Born to Hand-Jive" ....*Johnny Casino and Company*

Scene Two: FRONT OF BURGER PALACE

"Beauty School Dropout" ....*Teen Angel, Frenchy and Choir*

Scene Three: DRIVE-IN-MOVIE

"Alone at a Drive-In Movie" .... *Danny and Burger Palace Boys*

Scene Four: JAN'S PARTY

"Rock 'N' Roll Party Queen" ....*Doody and Roger*

"There Are Worse Things I Could Do"....................*Rizzo*

"'Look at Me, I'm Sandra Dee' Reprise".................. *Sandy*

Scene Five: INSIDE BURGER PALACE

"All Choked Up" .... *Sandy and Danny, Pink Ladies, Burger Palace Boys*

"'We Go Together' Reprise".....................*Entire Company*

CAST OF CHARACTERS

DANNY – The leader of the Burger Palace Boys. Well-built, nice-looking, with an air of cool easy-going charm. Strong and confident.

SANDY – Danny's love interest. Sweet, wholesome, naive, cute, like Sandra Dee of the "Gidget" movies.

THE PINK LADIES – The club-jacketed, gum-chewing, hip-swinging girls' gang that hangs around with the Burger Palace Boys

RIZZO – Leader of the Pink Ladies. She is tough, sarcastic and outspoken but vulnerable. Thin, Italian, with unconventional good looks.

FRENCHY – A dreamer. Good-natured and dumb. Heavily made-up, fussy about her appearance – particularly her hair. She can't wait to finish high school so she can be a beautician.

MARTY – The "beauty" of the Pink Ladies. Pretty, looks older than the other girls, but betrays her real age when she opens her mouth. Tries to act sophisticated.

JAN – Chubby, compulsive eater. Loud and pushy with the girls, but shy with boys.

THE BURGER PALACE BOYS – A super-cool, D.A.-haired, hard-looking group of high school wheeler-dealers…or so they think.

KENICKIE – Second-in-command of the Burger Palace Boys. Tough-looking, tattooed, surly, avoids any show of softness. Has an off-beat sense of humor.

DOODY – Youngest of the guys. Small, boyish, open, with a disarming smile and a hero-worshipping attitude toward the other guys. He also plays the guitar.

ROGER – The "anything-for-a-laugh" stocky type. Full of mischief, half-baked schemes and ideas. A clown who enjoys putting other people on.

SONNY – Italian-looking, with shiny black hair and dark oily skin. A braggart and wheeler-dealer who thinks he's a real lady-killer.

OTHER ROLES

PATTY – A typical cheerleader at a middle-class American public high school. Attractive and athletic. Aggressive, sure of herself, given to bursts of disconcerting enthusiasm. Catty, but in an All-American Girl sort of way. She can also twirl a baton.

CHA-CHA – A blind date. Slovenly, loud-mouthed and homely. Takes pride in being "the best dancer at St. Bernadette's."

EUGENE – The class valedictorian. Physically awkward, with weak eyes and a high-pitched voice. An apple-polisher, smug and pompous but gullible.

VINCE FONTAINE – A typical "teen audience" radio disc jockey. Slick, egotistical, fast-talking. A veteran "greaser."

JOHNNY CASINO – A "greaser" student at Rydell who leads a rock 'n' roll band and likes to think of himself as a real rock 'n' roll idol.

TEEN ANGEL – A good-looking falsetto-voiced, Fabian-look-alike. A singer who would have caused girls to scream and riot back in 1958.

MISS LYNCH – An old maid English teacher.

ACT ONE

Scene One

(Scene: Lights come up on the singing of the Rydell Alma Mater. Enter three people: **MISS LYNCH,** *an old maid English teacher who leads the singing;* **PATTY,** *former high school cheerleader and honor student [now a professional married career woman] and* **EUGENE FLORCZYK,** *former class valedictorian and honor student [now a vice-president of an advertising agency]. There is a large sign trimmed in green and brown behind them that reads:* "WELCOME BACK: RYDELL HIGH, CLASS' OF '59.")

[MUSIC NO. 1: RYDELL ALMA MATER]

ALL.

AS I GO TRAV'LING DOWN LIFE'S HIGHWAY
WHATEVER COURSE MY FORTUNES MAY FORETELL
I SHALL NOT GO ALONE ON MY WAY
FOR THOU SHALT ALWAYS BE WITH ME, RYDELL

WHEN I SEEK REST FROM WORLDLY MATTERS
IN PALACE OR IN HOVEL I MAY DWELL
AND THOUGH MY BED BE SILK OR TATTERS
MY DREAMS SHALL ALWAYS BE OF THEE, RYDELL

*(***EUGENE, PATTY** *and* **MISS LYNCH** *enter.)*

THROUGH ALL THE YEARS, RYDELL
AND TEARS, RYDELL
WE GIVE THREE CHEERS, RYDELL, FOR THEE
THROUGH EV'RYTHING, RYDELL
WE CLING, RYDELL
AND SING, RYDELL, TO THEE.

(As the songs ends, **MISS LYNCH** *introduces* **EUGENE** *and then takes her seat.)*

MISS LYNCH. Thank you. It is my pleasure at this time to introduce Mrs. Patricia Simcox Honeywell, your class yearbook editor, and Mr. Eugene Florczyk, class valedictorian and today vice-president of "Straight-Shooters" Unlimited, Research and Marketing.

EUGENE. Miss Lynch, fellow graduates, honored guests, and others. Looking over these familiar faces really takes me back to those wonderful bygone days. Days of working and playing together, days of cheering together for our athletic teams – Yay, Ringtails! – and days of worrying together when examination time rolled around. Perhaps some of those familiar faces of yesteryear are absent this evening because they thought our beloved Miss Lynch might have one of her famous English finals awaiting us. *(to* **MISS LYNCH***)* I was only joking. *(to audience)* However, the small portion of alumni I notice missing tonight are certainly not missing from our fond memories of them…and I'm sure they'd want us to know that they're fully present and accounted for in spirit, just the way we always remember them.

(School bell rings – "Chuck Berry" guitar run is heard. The **GREASERS** *are revealed in positions of laziness, defiance, boredom and amusement. They sing a parody of the "Alma Mater" as they take over the stage.)*

[MUSIC NO. 2: RYDELL ALMA MATER PARODY]

GREASERS.

I SAW A DEAD SKUNK ON THE HIGHWAY
AND I WAS GOIN' CRAZY FROM THE SMELL
'CAUSE WHEN THE WIND WAS BLOWIN' MY WAY
IT SMELLED JUST LIKE THE HALLS OF OLD RYDELL
AND IF YA' GOTTA USE THE TOILET
AND LATER ON YOU START TO SCRATCH LIKE HELL
TAKE OFF YOUR UNDERWEAR AND BOIL IT
'CAUSE YOU GOT MEMORIES OF OLD RYDELL.

I CAN'T EXPLAIN, RYDELL, THIS PAIN, RYDELL
IS IT PTOMAINE RYDELL GAVE ME?
IS IT V.D., RYDELL? COULD BE, RYDELL
YOU OUGHTA SEE THE FACULTY
IF MR. CLEAN, RYDELL, HAD SEEN RYDELL
HE'D JUST TURN GREEN AND DISAPPEAR
I'M OUTTA LUCK, RYDELL, DEAD DUCK, RYDELL
I'M STUCK, RYDELL, RIGHT HERE!

Scene Two

(Scene: The **GREASERS** *stalk off as the scene shifts to the high school cafeteria.* **JAN** *and* **MARTY** *enter, wearing their Pink Ladies jackets and carrying trays,* **JAN**'s *loaded with food. As each female character enters, she joins the others at one large table.)*

JAN. Jeez, I wish it was still summer. God, it's only a quarter after twelve and I feel like I been here a whole year already.

MARTY. Yeah, what a drag. Hey, you wanna sit here?

JAN. Yeah. Rizzo's coming and Frenchy's bringin' that new chick. Hey, Marty, who'd ya get for Economics? Old Man Drucker?

MARTY. Yeah, what a drag. He keeps makin' passes.

JAN. For real? He never tried nothin' with me!

MARTY. Huh. You want my coleslaw?

JAN. I'll see if I have room for it, *(***JAN** *takes coleslaw.)*

MARTY. Hey, Rizzo, over here!

*(***RIZZO** *enters carrying tray.)*

RIZZO. Hey, hey, hey! Hey, where's all the guys?

JAN. Those slobs. You think they'd spend a dime on their lunch? They're baggin' it.

RIZZO. Pretty cheap.

(Lights fade on the cafeteria, come up on **ROGER** *and* **DOODY** *sitting on the school steps.)*

DOODY. Hey, Rump, I'll trade ya a sardine for a liver sausage.

ROGER. I ain't eatin' one of those things. You had 'em in your ice box since last Easter.

DOODY. Nah, this was a fresh can. My ma just opened it this morning.

ROGER. You mean your old lady dragged her carcass out of bed for ya?

DOODY. Sure. She does it every year on the first day of school.

(KENICKIE *enters.*)

KENICKIE. Hey, where ya at?

ROGER. Hey, Kenickie. What's happening?

DOODY. Hey, Kenickie, whatcha got in the bag? I'll trade ya half a sardine.

KENICKIE. Get outta here with that dog food. I ain't messin' up my stomach with none of that crap. (KENICKIE *pulls a pack of Hostess Sno-Balls out of the bag and starts unwrapping it.*)

ROGER. Hey, Knicks, where were ya all summer?

KENICKIE. What are you, the F.B.I.?

ROGER. I was just askin'.

KENICKIE. I was workin'. Which is more than either of you two skids can say.

ROGER. Workin'! Yeah? Where?

KENICKIE. Luggin' boxes at Bargain City.

ROGER. Nice job!

KENICKIE. Hey, cramit! I'm savin' up to get me some wheels. That's the only reason I took the job.

ROGER. You gettin' a car, Kenick?

DOODY. Hey, cool! What kind?

KENICKIE. I don't know what kind yet, moron. But I got a name all picked out. "Greased Lightning"!

ROGER. (*putting him on*) Oh, nifty!

DOODY. Yeah. Maybe you oughtta get a hamster instead.

(DOODY *and* ROGER *laugh.*)

KENICKIE. Go ahead, laugh it up. When I show up in that baby, you suckers'll be laughin' out the other end.

ROGER. Will we ever!

(SONNY *enters, with wraparound sunglasses. As he enters, he pulls a class schedule out of his pocket.*)

KENICKIE. Hey, whattaya say, Sonny?

SONNY. Son of a "Bee." I got Old Lady Lynch for English again. She hates my guts. *(**SONNY** lights a cigarette.)*

ROGER. Nah, she's got the hots for ya, Sonny. That's why she keeps puttin' ya back in her class.

KENICKIE. Yeah, she's just waitin' for ya to grow up.

SONNY. Yeah, well, this year she's gonna wish she never seen me.

KENICKIE. Yeah? What are ya gonna do to her?

SONNY. I'm just not gonna take any of her crap, that's all. I don't take no crap from nobody.

*(**MISS LYNCH** enters.)*

MISS LYNCH. What's all the racket out here?

DOODY. Hi, Miss Lynch, did you have a nice summer?

*(**SONNY** hides his cigarette by cupping it in his hand and shoving his hand in his pocket.)*

SONNY. Hello, Miss Lynch, we was…uh…

MISS LYNCH. Dominic, aren't you supposed to be in class right now?

SONNY. I… I…

MISS LYNCH. You're just dawdling, aren't you? That's a fine way to start the new semester, Mr. LaTierri. Well? Are you going to stand there all day?

SONNY. No, Ma'am.

DOODY. No, Ma'am.

MISS LYNCH. Then move! *(**MISS LYNCH** exits.)*

SONNY. Yes, Ma'am. *(**SONNY** takes his hand out of his pocket and inhales on the still-burning cigarette.)*

ROGERS. I'm sure glad she didn't give you no crap, Son. You would have really told her off, right?

SONNY. Shaddup.

*(Lights fade on steps, come up again on **GIRLS** in the cafeteria.)*

MARTY. *(squinting and putting her rhinestone glasses on)* Hey, Jan, who's that chick with Frenchy? Is she the one you were tellin' me about?

JAN. Yeah, her name's Sandy. She seems pretty cool. Maybe we could let her in the Pink Ladies.

RIZZO. Just what we need. Another broad around.

(FRENCHY and SANDY enter, carrying trays.)

FRENCHY. Hi, you guys, this is my new next-door neighbor, Sandy Dumbrowski. This here's Rizzo and that's Marty and you remember Jan.

JAN. Sure. Hi.

SANDY. Hi. Pleased to meet you.

FRENCHY. *(to SANDY)* Come on, sit down. Hey, Marty, those new glasses?

MARTY. Yeah, I just got 'em for school. Do they make me look smarter?

RIZZO. Nah. We can still see your face.

MARTY. How'dja like rice pudding down your bra?

JAN. *I'll* take it! (**JAN** *reaches over and grabs the pudding.*)

RIZZO. How long you been livin' around here?

SANDY. Since July. My father just got transferred here.

MARTY. Hey, French, what'dja do to your hair. It really looks tough.

FRENCHY. Ah, I just touched it up a little.

JAN. You gonna eat your coleslaw, Sandy?

SANDY. It smells kinda funny.

(Diverting SANDY's attention. JAN grabs SANDY's coleslaw.)

FRENCHY. Wait'll you have the chipped beef. Better known as "Barf on a Bun."

MARTY. Don't mind her, Sandy. *Some* of us like to show off and use scurvy words.

RIZZO. *Some* of us? Check out Miss Toiletmouth over here.

MARTY. *(giving her "the finger")* Up yours, Rizzle!

JAN. *(trying to change the subject)* How do ya like the school so far, Sandy?

SANDY. Oh, it seems real nice. I was going to go to Immaculata, but my father had a fight with the Mother Superior over my patent leather shoes.

JAN. What do ya mean?

SANDY. She said boys could see up my dress in the reflection.

MARTY. Swear to God?

JAN. Hey, where do ya get shoes like that?

PATTY. *(offstage)* Hi, kids!

RIZZO. Hey, look who's comin'. Patty Simcox, the Little Lulu of Rydell High.

MARTY. Yeah. Wonder what she's doin' back here with us slobs?

RIZZO. Maybe she's havin' her period and wants to be alone.

(PATTY enters.)

PATTY. Well, don't say hello.

RIZZO. We won't.

PATTY. Is there room at your table?

MARTY. *(surprised)* Oh, yeah, move over, French.

PATTY. Oh, I just love the first day of school, don't you?

RIZZO. It's the biggest thrill of my life.

(FRENCHY starts doing RIZZO's hair.)

PATTY. You'll never guess what happened this morning.

RIZZO. Prob'ly not.

PATTY. Well, they announced this year's nominees for the Student Council, and guess who's up for vice president?

MARTY. *(knowing what's coming)* Who?

PATTY. Me! Isn't that wild?

RIZZO. Wild.

PATTY. I just hope I don't make *too* poor a showing.

RIZZO. Well, we sure wish ya all the luck in the world.

PATTY. Oh, uh, thanks. Oh, you must think I'm a terrible clod! I never even bothered to introduce myself to your new friend.

SANDY. Oh, I'm Sandy Dumbrowski.

PATTY. It's a real pleasure, Sandy. We certainly are glad to have you here at Rydell.

SANDY. Thank you.

PATTY. I'll bet you're going to be at the cheerleader try-outs next week, aren't you?

SANDY. Oh, no. I'd be too embarrassed.

PATTY. Don't be silly. I could give you a few pointers if you like.

MARTY. Aaaaaahhh, son of a bitch!

PATTY. Goodness gracious!

RIZZO. Nice language. What was that all about?

MARTY. (examining her glasses) One of my diamonds fell in the macaroni.

(Lights fade on GIRLS, come up on GUYS on the steps.)

DOODY. Hey, ain't that Danny over there?

SONNY. Where?

KENICKIE. Yeah. What's he doin' hangin' around the girls' gym entrance?

ROGER. Maybe he's hot for some chick!

SONNY. One of those skanks we've seen around since kindergarten? Not quite.

DOODY. (yells) HEY, DANNY! WHATCHA DOIN'?

ROGER. That's good, Dood. Play it real cool.

KENICKIE. Aw, leave him alone. Maybe he ain't gettin' any.

(DANNY enters, carrying books and lunch.)

DANNY. Hey, you guys, what's shakin'? (fakes SONNY out with a quick goose)

SONNY. Whattaya say, Zuko – 'dja see any good-lookin' stuff over there?

DANNY. Nah, just the same old chicks everybody's made it with!

DOODY. Where ya been all summer, Danny?

DANNY. Well, I spent a lot of time down at the beach.

KENICKIE. Hey, 'dja meet any new broads?

DANNY. Nah. Just met this one who was sorta cool, ya know?

SONNY. Ya mean she "goes all the way"?

DANNY. Is that all you ever think about, Sonny?

SONNY. *(looking around at the other* **GUYS***)* Friggin' A!

ROGER. Aahh, come off it, Zuko. Ya got "a little," right?

DANNY. Look, man. That's none of you guys' business.

KENICKIE. Okay, if that's the way you're gonna be.

DANNY. You don't want to hear all the horny details, anyway.

SONNY. *(starts tickling* **DANNY***)* Sure we do! Let's hear a little!

ROGER. *(joining in)* C'mon, Zuko, koochee koochee!

(All **GUYS** *join in playfully mauling* **DANNY** *as the lights fade on them and come back up on the* **GIRLS** *at the cafeteria table.)*

SANDY. I spent most of the summer at the beach.

JAN. What for? We got a brand new pool right in the neighborhood. It's real nice.

RIZZO. Yeah, if ya like swimmin' in Clorox.

SANDY. Well – actually, I met a boy there.

MARTY. You hauled your cookies all the way to the beach for some guy?

SANDY. This was sort of a special boy.

RIZZO. Are you kiddin'? There ain't no such thing.

(Lights stay up on **GIRLS***, come up on* **GUYS***.)*

[MUSIC NO. 3: SUMMER NIGHTS]

DANNY. Okay, you guys, ya wanna know what happened?

*(***GUYS** *say: Yea! Lets' hear it, etc.)*

SANDY. No, he was really nice. It was all very romantic.

(DANNY rises and sings "Summer Nights" to the GUYS. SANDY sings her version to the GIRLS.)

DANNY.

SUMMER LOVIN'! HAD ME A BLAST

SANDY.

SUMMER LOVIN'! HAPPENED SO FAST.

DANNY.

MET A GIRL CRAZY FOR ME

SANDY.

MET A BOY CUTE AS CAN BE

BOTH.

SUMMER DAY, DRIFTING AWAY, TO UH-OH, THOSE SUMMER
NIGHTS.

GUYS.

WELLA, WELLA, WELLA OOM
TELL ME MORE, TELL ME MORE

ROGER & DOODY.

DID YA GET VERY FAR?

GIRLS.

TELL ME MORE, TELL ME MORE

MARTY.

LIKE DOES HE HAVE A CAR?

(GUYS and GIRLS sing differing back-up.)

DANNY.

SHE SWAM BY ME, SHE GOT A CRAMP

SANDY.

HE RAN BY ME, GOT MY SUIT DAMP

DANNY.

SAVED HER LIFE, SHE NEARLY DROWNED

SANDY.

HE SHOWED OFF, SPLASHING AROUND

(Back-up ends.)

BOTH.

SUMMER SUN, SOMETHING BEGUN, THEN UH-OH, THOSE
SUMMER NIGHTS

GIRLS.

> WELLA, WELLA, WELL-UH HUH
>
> TELL ME MORE, TELL ME MORE

FRENCHY.

> WAS IT LOVE AT FIRST SIGHT?

GUYS.

> TELL ME MORE, TELL ME MORE

KENICKIE.

> DID SHE PUT UP A FIGHT?
>
> *(**GUYS** and **GIRLS** sing differing back-up.)*

DANNY.

> TOOK HER BOWLING, IN THE ARCADE

SANDY.

> WE WENT STROLLIN', DRANK LEMONADE

DANNY.

> WE MADE OUT, UNDER THE DOCK

SANDY.

> WE STAYED OUT TILL TEN O'CLOCK
>
> *(Back-up ends.)*

BOTH.

> SUMMER FLING, DON'T MEAN A THING, BUT, UH-OH, THOSE
> SUMMER NIGHTS

GUYS.

> WOH, WOH, WOH
>
> TELL ME MORE, TELL ME MORE, BUT YA DON'T HAVE TO
> BRAG

GIRLS.

> TELL ME MORE, TELL ME MORE.

RIZZO.

> 'CAUSE HE SOUNDS LIKE A DRAG
>
> *(**GUYS** and **GIRLS** sing differing back-up.)*

SANDY.

> HE GOT FRIENDLY, HOLDING MY HAND

DANNY.

> SHE GOT FRIENDLY, DOWN ON THE SAND

SANDY.

HE WAS SWEET, JUST TURNED EIGHTEEN

DANNY.

SHE WAS GOOD, YA KNOW WHAT I MEAN?

(Back-up ends.)

BOTH.

SUMMER HEAT, BOY AND GIRL MEET, THEN UH-OH, THOSE
SUMMER NIGHTS!

GIRLS.

WOH, WOH, WOH
TELL ME MORE, TELL ME MORE

JAN.

HOW MUCH DOUGH DID HE SPEND?

GUYS.

TELL ME MORE, TELL ME MORE

SONNY.

COULD SHE GET ME A FRIEND?

*(**GUYS** and **GIRLS** sing differing back-up.)*

SANDY.

IT TURNED COLDER, THAT'S WHERE IT ENDS

DANNY.

SO I TOLD HER WE'D STILL BE FRIENDS

SANDY.

THEN WE MADE OUR TRUE LOVE VOW

(Back-up ends.)

DANNY.

WONDER WHAT SHE'S DOIN' NOW

BOTH.

SUMMER DREAMS, RIPPED AT THE SEAMS, BUT, UH-OOH!
THOSE SUMMER NIGHTS!

GUYS & GIRLS.

TELL ME MORE, TELL ME MORE, OH –

(Lights stay up on both groups after song.)

PATTY. Gee, he sounds wonderful, Sandy.

DOODY. She really sounds cool, Danny.

RIZZO. A guy doesn't touch ya and it's true love. Maybe he was a pansy.

(SANDY *gives* RIZZO *a puzzled look.*)

ROGER. Big knockers, huh?

FRENCHY. Hey, nice talk, Rizzo!

KENICKIE. She Catholic?

JAN. What if we said that about Danny Zuko?

SONNY. Hot stuff, huh, Zuker?

SANDY. Did you say Danny Zuko?

DANNY. I didn't say that, Sonny!

RIZZO. Hey, was he the guy?

DOODY. Boy, you get all the "neats"!

SANDY. Doesn't he go to Lake Forest Academy?

(PINK LADIES *laugh.*)

KENICKIE. She doesn't go to Rydell, does she?

(DANNY *shakes his head "no."*)

MARTY. That's a laugh!

SONNY. Too bad, I'd bet she'd go for me.

PATTY. *(confidentially)* Listen, Sandy, forget Danny Zuko. I know some really sharp boys.

RIZZO. So do I. Right, you guys? C'mon, let's go.

(PINK LADIES *get up from the table,* SANDY *following them. The* GUYS *all laugh together.*)

FRENCHY. See ya 'round, Patty!

RIZZO. Yeah, maybe we'll drop in on the next Student Council meeting.

(RIZZO *nudges* MARTY *in the ribs. Lights go down on the lunchroom.* GIRLS *cross toward* GUYS *on steps.*)

MARTY. Well, speaking of the devil!

SONNY. *(to* GUYS*)* What'd I tell ya, they're always chasin' me.

MARTY. *(pushing* SONNY *away)* Not you, greaseball! Danny!

RIZZO. Yeah. We got a surprise for ya. (**PINK LADIES** *shove* **SANDY** *toward* **DANNY**.)

SANDY. *(surprised and nervous)* Hello, Danny.

DANNY. *(uptight)* Oh, hi. How are ya?

SANDY. Fine.

DANNY. Oh yeah...I...uh...thought you were goin' to Immaculata.

SANDY. I changed my plans.

DANNY. Yeah! Well, that's cool. I'll see ya around. Let's go, you guys. *(pushes* **GUYS** *out)*

DOODY. Where do you know her from, Danny?

DANNY. Huh? Oh, just an old friend of my family's.

SONNY. *(to* **DANNY***)* She's pretty sharp. I think she's got eyes for me, didja notice?

(**DANNY** *gives* **SONNY** *"a look," pulls him off. All* **GUYS** *exit.)*

JAN. *(picking up* **DANNY***'s lunch)* Gee, he was so glad to see ya, he dropped his lunch.

SANDY. I don't get it. He was so nice this summer.

FRENCHY. Don't worry about it, Sandy.

MARTY. Hey listen, how'd you like to come over to my house tonight? It'll be just us girls.

JAN. Yeah, those guys are all a bunch of creeps.

(**DANNY** *returns for his lunch.)*

RIZZO. Yeah, Zuko's the biggest creep of all.

(**RIZZO,** *seeing* **DANNY,** *exits. Other* **GIRLS** *follow.)*

[MUSIC NO. 3A: SCENE CHANGE 2]

Scene Three

(Scene: School bell rings and class change begins.
GREASERS, **PATTY** *and* **EUGENE** *enter, go to lockers, get*
books, etc. **DANNY** *sees* **DOODY** *with guitar.)*

DANNY. Hey, Doody, where'dja get the guitar?

DOODY. I just started takin' lessons this summer.

DANNY. Can you play anything on it?

DOODY. Sure. *(He fumbles with the frets and strikes a sour*
chord.) That's a "C." *(**DOODY** sits and waits for approval.)*

MARTY. *(baffled)* Hey, that's pretty good.

DOODY. *(hitting each chord)* Then I know an A minor, and an
F, and I've been workin' on a G.

FRENCHY. Hey! Can you play "Tell Laura I Love Her"?

DOODY. I don't know. Has it got a "C" in it?

DANNY. Hey, come on; let's hear a little, Elvis.

DOODY. *(pulling out instruction book)...* "Magic Changes," by
Ronny Dell... *(Sings off-key.)*
C-C-C-C-C
A-A-A-A MINOR
F-F-F-F-F-F
G-G-G-G SEVENTH

DANNY. That's terrific.

DOODY. Thanks – want to hear it again?

ALL. Sure! Yeah! *(etc.)*

*(**DOODY** starts to sing and other kids transform into*
rock 'n' roll, doo-wop group backing him as he suddenly
becomes a teen idol rock 'n' roll star.)

[MUSIC NO. 4: THOSE MAGIC CHANGES]

DOODY.
C-C-C-C-C
A-A-A-A MINOR
F-F-F-F-F-F
G-G-G-G SEVENTH

DOODY & GROUP.

C-C-C-C-C-C
A-A-A-A MINOR
F-F-F-F-F-F
G-G-G-G SEVENTH

DOODY.

WHAT'S THAT PLAYING ON THE RADIO?
WHY DO I START SWAYING TO AND FRO?
I HAVE NEVER HEARD THAT SONG BEFORE
BUT IF I DON'T HEAR IT ANY MORE
IT'S STILL FAMILIAR TO ME
SENDS A THRILL RIGHT THROUGH ME
'CAUSE THOSE CHORDS REMIND ME OF
THE NIGHT THAT I FIRST FELL IN LOVE TO
THOSE MAGIC CHANGES.

(**GUYS** and **GIRLS** underscore with "Ooh.")

MY HEART ARRANGES A MELODY

(**GUYS** and **GIRLS** underscore with "Ooh.")

THAT'S NEVER THE SAME
A MELODY
THAT'S CALLING YOUR NAME
AND BEGS YOU, PLEASE, COME BACK TO ME

(**DONNY** and **ROGER** underscore with "La, La, La.")

PLEASE RETURN TO ME
DON'T GO AWAY AGAIN
OH, MAKE THEM PLAY AGAIN
THE MUSIC I LONG TO HEAR
AS ONCE AGAIN YOU WHISPER IN MY EAR
OH, MY DARLIN' UH-HUH! (

GIRLS and **GUYS** underscore with "C,A,F,G.")

GIRLS & GUYS.

C-C-C-C-C-C
A-A-A-A MINOR
F-F-F-F-F-F
G-G-G-G SEVENTH

DOODY.

I'LL BE WAITING BY THE RADIO

(**GUYS** and **GIRLS** underscore.)

YOU'LL COME BACK TO ME SOME DAY I KNOW
BEEN SO LONESOME SINCE OUR LAST GOODBYE
BUT I'M SINGING AS I CRY-Y-Y
WHILE THE BASS IS SOUNDING
WHILE THE DRUMS APE POUNDING
BEATING OF MY BROKEN HEART
WILL CLIMB TO FIRST PLACE ON THE CHART
OHHH, MY HEART ARRANGES
OHHH, THOSE MAGIC CHANGES

C-C-C-C-C
A-A-A-A MINOR
F-F-F-F-F-F
G-G-G-G SEVENTH
SHOOP DOO WAH!

(At the end of the song, **MISS LYNCH** enters to break up the group. All exit, except **GUYS** and **SONNY**.)

MISS LYNCH. (to **SONNY**) Mr. LaTierri, aren't you due in Detention Hall right now?

(Guys all make fun of **SONNY** and lead him off to Detention hall.)

[MUSIC NO. 4A: SCENE CHANGE 3]

Scene Four

(Scene: A pajama party in MARTY's bedroom. MARTY, FRENCHY, JAN and RIZZO are in pastel baby doll pajamas, SANDY in a quilted robe buttoned all the way up to the neck. The WAXX jingle for The Vince Fontaine Show *is playing on the radio.)*

VINCE'S VOICE. Hey, hey, this is the main-brain, Vince Fontaine, at Big Fifteen! Spinnin' the stacks of wax, here at the House of Wax – W-A-X-X. *(OOO-ga horn sound)* Cruisin' time, 10:46. *(sound of ricocheting bullet)* Sharpshooter pick hit of the week. A brand new one shootin' up the charts like a rocket by "The Vel-doo Rays" – goin' out to Ronnie and Sheila, the kids down at Mom's school store, and especially to Little Joe and the LaDons – listen in while I give it a spin!

(Radio fades. FRENCHY is looking at a fan magazine that has a big picture of Fabian on the cover.)

FRENCHY. Hey, it says here that Fabian is in love with some Swedish movie star and might be gettin' married.

JAN. Oh, no!

MARTY. Who cares, as long as they don't get their hooks into "Kookie."

RIZZO. Hey, Frenchy, throw me a ciggie-butt, will ya?

(FRENCHY throws RIZZO a cigarette.)

MARTY. Me too, while ya got the pack out.

FRENCHY. Ya want one, Sandy?

SANDY. Oh, no thanks. I don't smoke.

FRENCHY. Ya don't? Didja ever try it?

SANDY. Well, no, but…

RIZZO. Go on, try it. It ain't gonna kill ya. Give her a Hit Parade!

(FRENCHY throws SANDY a Hit Parade.)

Now, when she holds up the match, suck in on it.

(**FRENCHY** *lights the cigarette,* **SANDY** *inhales and starts coughing violently.*)

RIZZO. *(cont.)* Oh, I shoulda told ya, don't inhale if you're not used to it.

MARTY. That's okay. You'll get better at it.

FRENCHY. Yeah, then I'll show ya how to French inhale. That's really cool. Watch. *(She demonstrates French inhaling.)*

JAN. Phtyyaaagghh! That's the ugliest thing I ever saw!

FRENCHY. Nah, the guys really go for it. That's how I got my nickname, Frenchy.

RIZZO. Sure it is. Jeez, you guys, I almost forgot! *(She removes ½ gallon of wine from her overnight bag.)* A little Sneaky Pete to get the party goin'.

JAN. Italian Swiss Colony. Wow, it's imported!

(**RIZZO** *passes bottle to* **MARTY**.)

FRENCHY. Hey, we need some glasses.

RIZZO. Just drink it out of the bottle, we ain't got cooties.

MARTY. It's kind of sweet. I think I like Thunderbird better.

RIZZO. Okay, Princess Grace.

(**RIZZO** *takes bottle away from* **MARTY**)

MARTY. *(grabbing bottle back)* I didn't say I didn't want any, it just don't taste very strong, that's all.

(**MARTY** *passes bottle to* **SANDY**, *who quickly passes it to* **JAN**.)

JAN. Hey, I brought some Twinkies, anybody want one?

MARTY. Twinkies and wine? That's real class, Jan.

JAN. *(pointing to label on bottle)* It says right here, it's a dessert wine!

(**JAN** *passes wine to* **FRENCHY**.)

RIZZO. Hey, Sandy didn't get any wine.

(**RIZZO** *hands bottle to* **SANDY**.)

SANDY. Oh, that's okay. I don't mind.

RIZZO. Hey, I'll bet you never had a drink before, either...

SANDY. Sure I did. I had some champagne at my cousin's wedding once.

RIZZO. Oh, Ring-a-ding-ding.

(RIZZO *hands her wine.* SANDY *sips wine cautiously.*)

Hey, no! Ya gotta chug it. Like this! (RIZZO *takes a big slug from the bottle.*) Otherwise you swallow air bubbles and that's what makes you throw up.

JAN. I never knew that.

MARTY. Sure, Rudy from the Capri Lounge told me the same thing.

(SANDY *takes a slug from the bottle and holds it in her mouth trying to swallow it.*)

JAN. Hey, Sandy, you ever wear earrings? I think they'd keep your face from lookin' so skinny.

MARTY. Hey! Yeah! I got some big round ones made out of real mink. They'd look great on you.

FRENCHY. Wouldja like me to pierce your ears for ya, Sandy? I'm gonna be a beautician, y'know.

JAN. Yeah, she's real good. She did mine for me.

SANDY. Oh no, my father'd probably kill me.

MARTY. You still worry about what your old man thinks?

SANDY. Well...no. But isn't it awfully dangerous?

RIZZO. (*leans down to* SANDY) You ain't afraid, are ya?

SANDY. Of course not!

FRENCHY. Good. Hey, Marty, you got a needle around?

(FRENCHY *rummages in dresser for needle.*)

MARTY. Hey, how about my virgin pin!

(MARTY *reaches for her Pink Ladies jacket and takes off "circle pin" handing it to* FRENCHY.)

JAN. Nice to know it's good for somethin'.

MARTY. What's that crack supposed to mean?

JAN. Forget it, Marty, I was just teasing ya.

MARTY. Yeah, well, tease somebody else. It's my house.

(FRENCHY *begins to pierce* SANDY'*s ears.* SANDY *yelps.*)

FRENCHY. Hey, would ya hold still!

MARTY. *(to the rescue)* Hey, French...why don't you take Sandy in the John? My old lady'd kill me if we got blood all over the rug.

SANDY. Huh?

FRENCHY. It only bleeds for a second. Come on.

JAN. Aaaww! We miss all the fun! (JAN *opens a second package of Twinkies as* FRENCHY *begins to lead* SANDY *off.*)

FRENCHY. Hey, Marty, I need some ice to numb her earlobes.

MARTY. *(exasperated)* Ahh...look, why don'tcha just let the cold water run for a little while, then stick her ear under the faucet?

SANDY. Listen, I'm sorry, but I'm not feeling too well, and I...

RIZZO. Look, Sandy, if you think you're gonna be hangin' around with the Pink Ladies – you gotta get with it! Otherwise, forget it...and go back to your hot cocoa and Girl Scout cookies!

SANDY. Okay, come on...Frenchy.

JAN. Hey, Sandy, don't sweat it. If she screws up, she can always fix your hair so your ears won't show.

FRENCHY. Har-dee-har-har!

RIZZO. That chick's gettin' to be a real nerd.

JAN. Ah, lay off, Rizzo.

MARTY. Yeah, she can't help it if she ain't been around.

RIZZO. Yeah, well, how long are we supposed to play babysitter for her?

(Suddenly a loud "urp" sound is heard offstage.)

What was that?

(The girls all look at each other, bewildered for a couple of seconds, then FRENCHY *runs back into the room.)*

FRENCHY. Hey, Marty, Sandy's sick. She's heavin' all over the place!

JAN. 'Dja do her ears already?

FRENCHY. Nah. I only did one. As soon as she saw the blood she went BLEUGH!

RIZZO. God! What a Party Poop!

(MARTY *pulls out a gaudy kimono. She makes a big show of putting it on.*)

MARTY. Jeez, it's gettin' kinda chilly. I think I'll put my robe on.

JAN. Hey, Marty, where'dja get that thing?

MARTY. Oh, you like it? It's from Japan.

RIZZO. Yeah, everything's made in Japan these days.

MARTY. No, this guy I know sent it to me.

FRENCHY. No kiddin'!

JAN. You goin' with a Jap?

MARTY. He ain't a Jap, stupid. He's a Marine. And, a real doll, too.

FRENCHY. Oh, wow! Hey, Marty, can he get me one of those things?

JAN. You never told us you knew any Marines.

RIZZO. How long you known this guy?

MARTY. Oh…just a couple of months. I met him on a blind date at the roller rink…and the next thing I know, he joins up. Anyway, right off the bat he starts sendin' me things – and then today I got this kimono. *(trying to be cool)* Oh yeah, look what else! (MARTY *takes a ring out of cleavage.*)

FRENCHY. Oh, neat!

MARTY. It's just a tiny bit too big. So I gotta get some angora for it.

FRENCHY. Jeez! Engaged to a Marine!

RIZZO. *(sarcastically)* Endsville.

JAN. What's this guy look like, Marty?

FRENCHY. You got a picture?

MARTY. Yeah, but it's not too good. He ain't in uniform. (**MARTY** *takes her wallet out of the dresser. It's one of those fat bulging ones with rubber bands around it. She swings wallet and accordion picture folder drops to floor.*) Oh, here it is… next to Paul Anka.

JAN. How come it's ripped in half?

MARTY. Oh, his old girl friend was in the picture.

JAN. What's this guy's name, anyway?

MARTY. Oh! It's Freddy. Freddy Strulka.

JAN. He a Polack?

MARTY. Naah, I think he's Irish.

FRENCHY. Do you write him a lot, Marty?

MARTY. Pretty much. Every time I get a present.

JAN. Whattaya say to a guy in a letter, anyway?

(**MARTY** *and* **GIRLS** *suddenly become a rock 'n' roll singing quartet.*)

[MUSIC NO. 5: FREDDY, MY LOVE]

MARTY. *(sings)*

FREDDY, MY LOVE, I MISS YOU MORE THAN WORDS CAN SAY

(**GIRLS** *sing back-up throughout.*)

FREDDY, MY LOVE, PLEASE KEEP IN TOUCH WHILE YOU'RE
    AWAY
HEARING FROM YOU CAN MAKE THE DAY SO MUCH BETTER
GETTING A SOUVENIR OR MAYBE A LETTER
I REALLY FLIPPED OVER THE GREY CASHMERE SWEATER
FREDDY, MY LOVE
(FREDDY, MY LOVE, FREDDY, MY LOVE, FREDDY MY LO-OOVE)

FREDDY, YOU KNOW, YOUR ABSENCE MAKES ME FEEL SO
    BLUE
THAT'S OKAY, THOUGH, YOUR PRESENTS MAKE ME THINK
    OF YOU
MY MA WILL HAVE A HEART ATTACK WHEN SHE CATCHES
THOSE PEDAL PUSHERS WITH THE BLACK LEATHER
    PATCHES
OH, HOW I WISH I HAD A JACKET THAT MATCHES

FREDDY, MY LOVE
(FREDDY, MY LOVE, FREDDY, MY LOVE, FREDDY, MY LO-OOVE)

DON'T KEEP YOUR LETTERS FROM ME
I THRILL TO EVERY LINE
YOUR SPELLING'S KINDA CRUMMY
BUT HONEY, SO IS MINE
I TREASURE EVERY GIFTIE
THE RING IS REALLY NIFTY
YOU SAY IT COST YOU FIFTY
SO YOU'RE THRIFTY,
I DON'T MIND!

FREDDY, YOU'LL SEE, YOU'LL HOLD ME IN YOUR ARMS
    SOMEDAY
AND I WILL BE WEARING YOUR LACY LINGERIE
THINKING ABOUT IT, MY HEART'S POUNDING ALREADY
KNOWING WHEN YOU COME HOME WE'RE BOUND TO GO
    STEADY
AND THROW YOUR SERVICE PAY AROUND LIKE CONFETTI
FREDDY, MY LOVE
(FREDDY, MY LOVE, FREDDY, MY LOVE, FREDDY, MY LO-OOVE)
(FREDDY, MY LOVE, FREDDY, MY LOVE, FREDDY, MY LO-OOVE)
(FREDDY, MY LOVE, FREDDY, MY LOVE, FREDDY, MY LO-OOVE)
(FREDDY, MY LOVE, FREDDY, MY LOVE, FREDDY, MY LO-OOVE)

(On the last few bars of song the **GIRLS** *fall asleep one by one, until* **RIZZO** *is the only one left awake. She pulls pants on over her pajamas and climbs out the window. Just at that moment,* **SANDY** *comes back into the room unnoticed by* **RIZZO**. **SANDY** *stands looking after her.)*

Scene Five

(Scene: **GUYS** *come running on out of breath, and carrying quarts of beer and four hubcaps.* **DANNY** *has tire iron.)*

DANNY. I don't know why I brought this tire iron! I coulda yanked these babies off with my bare hands!

SONNY. Sure ya could, Zuko! I just broke six fingernails!

ROGER. Hey, you guys, these hubcaps ain't got a scratch on 'em. They must be worth two beans a piece easy.

DOODY. No kiddin'? Hey, how much can we get for these dice? *(pulls out foam rubber dice)*

ROGER. Hey, who the hell would put brand new chromers on a second-hand Dodgem car!

DANNY. Probably some real tool!

SONNY. Hey, c'mon, let's go push these things off on somebody!

DANNY. Eleven o'clock at night? Sure, maybe we could go sell 'em at a police station!

DOODY. A police station, what a laugh! They don't use these kinda hubcaps on cop cars.

(A car horn is heard.)

SONNY. Hey, here comes that car we just hit! Let's make tracks! Ditch the evidence!

*(**GUYS** run, dropping hubcaps. **SONNY** tries to scoop them up as **KENICKIE** drives on in "Greased Lightning.")*

DANNY. Hey, wait a minute – it's Kenickie!

KENICKIE. All right, put those things back on the car, dipstick!

SONNY. Jeez, whatta grouch! We was only holdin' 'em for ya so nobody'd swipe 'em.

DOODY. *(handing back dice)* Hey, where'dja get these cool dice?

DANNY. Kenickie, whattaya doin' with this hunk-ah-junk, anyway?

KENICKIE. Whattaya mean? This is "Greased Lightning"!

("Whats" and puzzled looks go up from GUYS.)

SONNY. What? You really expect to make out in this sardine can?

KENICKIE. Hey, get bent, LaTierri!

ROGERS. Nice color, what is it? Candy Apple Primer?

KENICKIE. That's all right – wait till I give it a paint job and soup up the engine – she'll work like a champ!

DANNY. *(looking at car and picking up mike)* The one and only Greased Lightning!

(Driving guitar begins playing.)

[MUSIC NO. 6: GREASED LIGHTNIN']

KENICKIE. *(sings)*

I'LL HAVE ME OVERHEAD LIFTERS AND FOUR-BARREL
QUADS, OH, YEAH

(GUYS sing back-up throughout.)

A FUEL-INJECTION CUT-OFF AND CHROME-PLATED RODS,
OH, YEAH
WITH A FOUR-SPEED ON THE FLOOR, THEY'LL BE WAITIN'
AT THE DOOR
YA KNOW WITHOUT A DOUBT, I'LL BE REALLY MAKIN' OUT
IN GREASED LIGHTNIN'!

KENICKIE.

GO, GREASED LIGHTNIN', YOU'RE BURNIN' UP THE
QUARTER MILE

GUYS.

GREASED LIGHTNIN', GO, GREASED LIGHTNIN'

KENICKIE.

YEAH, GREASED LIGHTNIN', YOU'RE COASTIN' THROUGH
THE HEAT-LAP TRIALS

GUYS.

GREASED LIGHTNIN', YEAH, GREASED LIGHTNIN'

KENICKIE.

YOU ARE SUPREME

GUYS.

UH-HUH

KENICKIE.

THE CHICKS'LL DREAM

GUYS.

UH-HUH

KENICKIE.

'BOUT GREASED LIGHTNIN'!

GUYS.

GO, GO, GO, GO,

GO, GO, GO, GO, GO, GO, GO, GO

KENICKIE.

I'LL HAVE ME PURPLE FRENCHED TAIL-LIGHTS AND THIRTY-
INCH FINS, OH YEAH

*(**GUYS** sing back-up throughout.)*

A PALOMINO DASHBOARD AND DUAL MUFFLER TWINS, OH
YEAH

WITH NEW PISTONS, PLUGS, AND SHOCKS, SHE CAN BEAT
THE SUPER-STOCKS

YA KNOW THAT I AIN'T BRAGGIN', SHE'S A REAL DRAGGIN'
WAGON.

GREASED LIGHTNIN'!

KENICKIE.

GO, GREASED LIGHTNIN', YOU'RE BURNIN' UP THE
QUARTER MILE

GUYS.

GREASED LIGHTNIN', GO, GREASED LIGHTNIN'

KENICKIE.

YEAH, GREASED LIGHTNIN', YOU'RE COASTIN' THROUGH
THE HEAT-LAP TRIALS

GUYS.

GREASED LIGHTNIN', YEAH, GREASED LIGHTNIN'

KENICKIE.

YOU ARE SUPREME

GUYS.

UH-HUH

KENICKIE.

THE CHICKS'LL DREAM

GUYS.

UH-HUH

KENICKIE.

'BOUT GREASED LIGHTNIN'!

GUYS.

GO, GO, GO, GO,

GO, GO, GO, GO, GO, GO, GO, GO

(dance break)

GUYS.

GO, GO, GO, GO,

GO, GO, GO, GO, GO, GO, GO, GO

KENICKIE.

GO, GREASED LIGHTNIN', YOU'RE BURNIN' UP THE
    QUARTER MILE

GUYS.

GREASED LIGHTNIN', GO, GREASED LIGHTNIN'

KENICKIE.

YEAH, GREASED LIGHTNIN', YOU'RE COASTIN' THROUGH
    THE HEAT-LAP TRIALS

GUYS.

GREASED LIGHTNIN', YEAH, GREASED LIGHTNIN'

KENICKIE.

YOU ARE SUPREME

GUYS.

UH-HUH

KENICKIE.

THE CHICKS'LL DREAM

GUYS.

UH-HUH

KENICKIE.

FOR GREASED LIGHTNIN'!

GUYS.

LIGHTNIN', LIGHTNIN' LIGHTNIN'

(As song ends, **RIZZO** *enters.)*

RIZZO. What is that thing?

KENICKIE. Hey, what took you so long?

RIZZO. Never mind what took me so long. Is that your new custom convert?

KENICKIE. This is it! Ain't it cool?

RIZZO. Yeah, it's about as cool as a Good Humor truck.

KENICKIE. Okay, Rizzo, if that's how you feel, why don'tcha go back to the pajama party? Plenty of chicks would get down on their knees to ride around in this little number.

RIZZO. Sure they would! Out! What do ya think this is, a gang bang?

*(***RIZZO*** *opens the passenger door, shoving* **GUYS** *out.)*

Hey, Danny! I just left your girlfriend at Marty's house, flashin' all over the place.

DANNY. Whattaya talkin' about?

RIZZO. Sandy Dumbrowski! Y'know…Sandra Dee.

KENICKIE. Be cool, you guys.

*(***RIZZO*** *immediately starts crawling all over* **KENICKIE.***)*

DANNY. Hey, you better tell that to Rizzo I –

(siren sounds)

KENICKIE. The fuzz! Hey, you guys better get ridda those hubcaps.

DANNY. Whattaya mean, man? They're yours!

*(***GUYS*** *throw hubcaps on car hood.)*

KENICKIE. Oh no, they're not. I stole 'em.

(**KENICKIE** *starts to drive off. Siren sounds again. All* **GUYS** *leap on car, drive off, singing: "Go Greased Lightning," etc., as the lights change to new scene.*)

[MUSIC NO. 6A: GREASED LIGHTNIN' – RIZZO'S ENTRANCE]

KENICKIE & GROUP.

GREASED LIGHTNIN'! GO GREASED LIGHTNIN'
GREASED LIGHTNIN'! GO GREASED LIGHTNIN'
GREASED LIGHTNIN'! GO GREASED LIGHTNIN'

Scene Six

(Scene: **SANDY** *runs on with pom poms, dressed in a green baggy gym suit. She does a Rydell cheer.)*

SANDY. Do a split, give a yell

Throw a fit for old Rydell

Way to go, green and brown

Turn the foe upside down.

*(***SANDY*** *does awkward split.* **DANNY** *enters.)*

DANNY. Hiya, Sandy.

*(***SANDY*** *gives him a look and turns her head so that* **DANNY** *sees the Band-Aid on her ear.)*

Hey, what happened to your ear?

SANDY. Huh? *(She covers her ear with her hand, answers coldly.)* Oh, nothing. Just an accident.

DANNY. Hey, look, uh, I hope you're not bugged about that first day at school. I mean, couldn't ya tell I was glad to see ya?

SANDY. Well, you could've been a little nicer to me in front of your friends.

DANNY. Are you kidding? Hey, you don't know those guys. They just see ya talkin' to a chick and right away they think she puts…well, you know what I mean.

SANDY. I'm not sure. It looked to me like maybe you had a new girlfriend or something.

DANNY. Are you kiddin'! Listen, if it was up to me, I'd never even look at any other chick but you.

*(***SANDY*** *blushes.)*

Hey, tell ya what. We're throwin' a party in the park tomorrow night for Frenchy. She's gonna quit school before she flunks again and go to Beauty School. How'dja like to make it on down there with me?

SANDY. I'd really like to, but I'm not so sure those girls want me around anymore.

DANNY. Listen, Sandy. Nobody's gonna start gettin' salty with ya when I'm around. Uh-uhh!

SANDY. All right, Danny, as long as you're with me. Let's not let anyone come between us again, okay?

PATTY. *(rushing onstage with two batons and wearing cheer-leader outfit)* HHIIiiiiii, Danny! Oh, don't let me interrupt.

(gives SANDY baton) Here, why don't you twirl this for awhile.

(taking DANNY aside) I've been dying to tell you something. You know what I found out after you left my house the other night? My mother thinks you're cute. *(to SANDY)* He's such a lady-killer.

SANDY. Isn't he, though! *(out of corner of mouth, to DANNY)* What were you doing at her house?

DANNY. Ah, I was just copying down some homework.

PATTY. Come on, Sandy, let's practice.

SANDY. Yeah, let's! I'm just dying to make a good impression on all those cute lettermen.

DANNY. Oh, that's why you're wearing that thing – gettin' ready to show off your skivvies to a bunch of horny jocks?

SANDY. Don't tell me you're jealous, Danny.

DANNY. What? Of that bunch ah meatheads! Don't make me laugh. Ha! Ha!

SANDY. Just because they can do something you can't do?

DANNY. Yeah, sure, right.

SANDY. Okay, what have *you* ever done?

DANNY. *(to PATTY, twirling baton)* Stop that! *(thinking a moment)* I won a Hully-Gully contest at the "Teen-Talent" record hop.

SANDY. Aaahh, you don't even know what I'm talking about.

DANNY. Whattaya mean, look, I could run circles around those jerks.

SANDY. But you'd rather spend your time copying other people's homework.

DANNY. Listen, the next time they have tryouts for any of those teams I'll show you what I can do.

PATTY. Oh, what a lucky coincidence! The track team's having tryouts tomorrow.

DANNY. *(panic)* Huh? Okay, I'll be there.

SANDY. Big talk.

DANNY. You think so, huh. Hey, Patty, when'dja say those tryouts were?

PATTY. Tomorrow, tenth period on the football field.

DANNY. Good, I'll be there. You're gonna come watch me, aren't you?

PATTY. Ooohh, I can't wait!

DANNY. Solid. I'll see ya there, sexy. *(DANNY exits.)*

PATTY. Toodles! *(elated, turns to SANDY)* Ooohh, I'm so excited, aren't you?

SANDY. Come on, let's practice.

(They sing "Rydell Fight Song," twirling batons, SANDY just missing PATTY's head with each swing.)

[MUSIC NO. 7: RYDELL FIGHT SONG]

SANDY & PATTY.

HIT 'EM AGAIN, RYDELL RINGTAILS
TEAR 'EM APART, GREEN AND BROWN
BASH THEIR BRAINS OUT, STOMP 'EM ON THE FLOOR
FOR THE GLORY OF RYDELL EVER MORE.

FIGHT TEAM, FIGHT, FIGHT, TEAM FIGHT
CHEW 'EM UP – SPIT 'EM OUT
FIGHT TEAM, FIGHT.

(SANDY and PATTY exit doing majorette march step.)

Scene Seven

(Scene: A deserted section of the park. **JAN** *and* **ROGER** *on picnic table.* **RIZZO** *and* **KENICKIE** *making out on bench.* **MARTY** *sitting on other bench.* **FRENCHY** *and* **SONNY** *on blanket reading fan magazines.* **DANNY** *pacing.* **DOODY** *sitting on a trash can. A portable radio is playing* The Vince Fontaine Show.*)*

VINCE'S RADIO VOICE. Hey, gettin' bark on the rebound here for our second half. *(cuckoo sound)* Dancin' Word Bird Contest comin' up in a half hour, when maybe I'll call you. Hey, I think you'll like this little ditty from the city, a new group discovered by Alan Freed. Turn up the sound and stomp on the ground. Ooohh, yeah!!!

(Radio fades.)

DANNY. Hey, Frenchy, when do ya start beauty school?

FRENCHY. Next week. I can hardly wait. No more dumb books and stupid teachers.

MARTY. *(holding out a package of Vogues)* Hey, anybody want a Vogue?

FRENCHY. Yeah, you got any pink ones left?

SONNY. Yeah, give me one. *(puts it in his mouth)* How about one for later?

MARTY. *(throwing him another cigarette)* God, what a mooch!

DOODY. Hey, Rump. You shouldn't be eatin' that cheeseburger. It's still Friday, y'know!

ROGER. Ah, for cryin' out loud. What'dja remind me for? Now I gotta go to confession. *(He takes another bite of the cheeseburger.)*

JAN. Well, I can eat anything. That's the nice thing about bein' a Lutheran.

ROGER. Yeah, that's the nice thing about bein' Petunia Pig.

JAN. *(giving* **ROGER** *the finger)* Look who's talkin' Porky.

FRENCHY. Hey, Sonny, don't maul that magazine. There's a picture of Ricky Nelson in there I really wanna save.

SONNY. I was just lookin' at Shelley Farberay's jugs.

(FRENCHY *leans over to look at picture.*)

FRENCHY. *(primping)* Y'know, lotsa people think I look just like Shelley Farberries.

SONNY. Not a chance. You ain't got a "set" like hers.

FRENCHY. I happen to know she wears falsies.

SONNY. You oughtta know, Foam-Domes.

JAN. You want another cheeseburger?

ROGER. Nah, I think I'll have a Coke.

JAN. You shouldn't drink so much Coke. It rots your teeth.

ROGER. Thank you, Bucky Beaver.

JAN. I ain't kiddin'. Somebody told me about this scientist once who knocked out one of his teeth and dropped it in this glass of Coke, and after a week, the tooth rotted away until there was nothing left.

ROGER. For Christ sake, I ain't gonna carry a mouthful of Coke around for a week. Besides, what do you care what I do with my teeth? It ain't your problem.

JAN. No, I guess not.

MARTY. *(wearing extra-large college letterman sweater and modeling for* DANNY*)* Hey, Danny, how would I look as a college girl?

DANNY. *(pulling sweater tight)* Boola-Boola...

MARTY. Hey, watch it! It belongs to this big Jock at Holy Contrition.

DANNY. *(indicating* MARTY*'s sweater)* Wait'll ya see me wearin' one of those things. I tried out for the track team today.

(*Several heads turn and look at* DANNY. *Ad libs of: What? Zuko, not, etc.*)

MARTY. Are you serious? With those bird legs?

(*Kids all laugh.* ROGER *does funny imitation of* DANNY *as a gung-ho track star.*)

DANNY. Hey, better hobby than yours, Rump.

(Other guys laugh at remark, all giving **ROGER** *calls of "Rump-Rump?")*

JAN. *(after a pause)* How come you never get mad at those guys?

ROGER. Why should I?

JAN. Well, that name they call you. Rump!

ROGER. That's just my nickname. It's sorta like a title.

JAN. Whattaya mean?

ROGER. I'm king of the mooners.

JAN. The what?

ROGER. I'm the mooning champ of Rydell High.

JAN. You mean showm' off your bare behind to people? That's pretty raunchy.

ROGER. Nah, it's neat! I even mooned old Lady Lynch once. I hung one on her right out the car window. And she never even knew who it was.

JAN. Too much! I wish I'd been there. *(quickly)* I mean... y'know what I mean.

ROGER. Yeah. I wish you'd been there, too.

JAN. *(seriously)* You do?

*(**ROGER** answers her by singing.)*

[MUSIC NO. 8: MOONING]

ROGER.
I SPEND MY DAYS JUST MOONING
SO SAD AND BLUE
I SPEND MY NIGHTS JUST MOONING
ALL OVER YOU.

JAN.
ALL OVER WHO?

ROGER.
OH, I'M SO FULL OF LOVE (**JAN** *oohs underneath.)*
AS ANY FOOL CAN SEE
'CAUSE ANGELS UP ABOVE
HAVE HUNG A MOON ON ME.

JAN.

WHY MUST YOU GO?

ROGER.

WHY MUST I GO ON MOONING
SO ALL ALONE
THERE WOULD BE NO MORE MOONING
IF YOU WOULD CALL ME

JAN.

UP ON THE PHONE

ROGER.

I GUESS I'LL KEEP ON STRIKING POSES
TILL MY CHEEKS HAVE LOST THEIR ROSES.
MOONING OVER YOU
I'LL STAND BEHIND YOU MOONING
FOREVER MORE.

JAN.

FOR EVERMORE

ROGER & JAN.

SOMEDAY YOU'LL (I'LL) FIND ME MOONING
AT YOUR FRONT DOOR

JAN.

AT MY FRONT DOOR

ROGER.

OH, EVERY DAY AT SCHOOL I WATCH YA
ALWAYS WILL UNTIL I GOTCHA

ROGER & JAN.

MOONING, TOO.

ROGER.

THERE'S A MOON OUT TONIGHT

DOODY. *(loudly)* Hey, Danny, there's that chick ya know.

(**SANDY** *and* **EUGENE** *enter.* **EUGENE** *wearing Bermuda shorts and argyle socks. They both have bags with leaves.* **RIZZO** *and* **KENICKIE** *sit up to look.* **DANNY** *moves to* **EUGENE** *and stares him down.)*

EUGENE. Well, Sandy, I think I have all the leaves I want. Uh…why don't I wait for you with dad in the station wagon.

(DANNY *looking at* EUGENE *outlines a square with jerking head movement.* EUGENE *exits. As* DANNY *walks away,* SONNY *crosses to* SANDY.)

SONNY. Hi ya, Sandy. What's shakin'? How 'bout a beer?

SANDY. (*giving* DANNY *a look*) No, thanks, I can't stay.

DANNY. Oh, yeah? Then whattaya doin' hangin' around?

(DANNY *casually puts his hand on* MARTY*'s shoulder and* MARTY *looks at him, bewildered.*)

SANDY. I just came out to collect some leaves for Biology.

SONNY. Oh, yeah? There's some really neat yellow ones over by the drainage canal. C'mon, I'll show ya'!

(SONNY *grabs* SANDY *and goes offstage.*)

KENICKIE. (*shouting*) Those ain't leaves. They're used balloons.

DOODY. Hey, Danny…ain't you gonna follow 'em?

DANNY. Why should I? She don't mean nothin' to me.

RIZZO. (*to* DANNY) Sure, Zuko, every day now! Ya mean you ain't told 'em?

KENICKIE. Told us what?

RIZZO. Oh, nothin'. Right, Zuko?

KENICKIE. Come off it, Rizzo. Whattaya' tryin' to do, make us think she's like you?

RIZZO. What's that crack supposed to mean? I ain't heard you complainin'.

KENICKIE. That's 'cause ya been stuck to my face all night.

DANNY. Hey, cool it, huh?

RIZZO. Yeah, Kenickie, if you don't shut up you're gonna get a knuckle sandwich.

KENICKIE. Ohh, I'm really worried, scab!

RIZZO. Okay, you bastard!

(*She pushes him off bench and they fight on ground.*)

ROGER & DOODY. Fight! Fight! Yaaayy! *(etc.)*

DANNY. *(separating them)* Come on, cut it out!

> *(**RIZZO** and **KENICKIE** stop fighting and glare at each other.)*

What a couple of fruitcakes!

RIZZO. Well, he started it.

KENICKIE. God, what a yo-yo! Make one little joke and she goes tutti-frutti *(**KENICKIE** sulks over to garbage can.)*

DOODY. Jeez, nice couple.

> *(There is an uncomfortable pause onstage as the kids hear **VINCE FONTAINE** on radio.)*

VINCE'S VOICE. ...'cause tomorrow night yours truly, the main-brain, Vince Fontaine, will be emceeing the big dance bash out at Rydell High School – in the boys' gym, and along with me will be Mr. T.N.T. himself, Johnny Casino and the Gamblers. So, make it a point to stop by the joint, Rydell High, 7:30 tomorrow night.

RIZZO. Hey, Danny, you goin' to the dance tomorrow night?

DANNY. I don't think so.

RIZZO. Awww, you're all broke up over little Gidget!

DANNY. Who?

RIZZO. Ahh, c'mon, Zuko, why don'tcha take me to the dance – I can pull that Sandra Dee crap, too. Right, you guys?

> *(**ROGER** and **DOODY** do MGM lion. **RIZZO** sings.)*

[MUSIC NO. 9: LOOK AT ME, I'M SANDRA DEE]

RIZZO.

> LOOK AT ME, I'M SANDRA DEE
> LOUSY WITH VIRGINITY
> WON'T GO TO BED TILL I'M LEGALLY WED
> I CAN'T, I'M SANDRA DEE
>
> WATCH IT, HEY, I'M DORIS DAY
> I WAS NOT BROUGHT UP THAT WAY
> WON'T COME ACROSS, EVEN ROCK HUDSON LOST

HIS HEART TO DORIS DAY.

I DON'T DRINK OR SWEAR
I DON'T RAT MY HAIR
I GET ILL FROM ONE CIGARETTE
KEEP YOUR FILTHY PAWS OFF MY SILKY DRAWERS
WOULD YOU PULL THAT STUFF WITH ANNETTE?

(**SANDY** *and* **SONNY** *enter, hearing the last part of the song.* **SONNY** *is behind her.*)

AS FOR YOU, TROY DONAHUE
I KNOW WHAT YOU WANNA DO
YOU GOT YOUR CRUST, I'M NO OBJECT OF LUST
I'M JUST PLAIN SANDRA DEE.

NO, NO, NO, SAL MINEO
I COULD NEVER STOOP SO LOW
PLEASE KEEP YOUR COOL, NOW YOU'RE STARTING TO
    DROOL
FONGOOL
I'M SANDRA DEE!

(**SANDY** *crosses to* **RIZZO**.)

SONNY. Hey, Sandy, wait a minute...hey...

SANDY. *(to* **RIZZO**) Listen, just who do you think you are? I saw you making fun of me.

(**SANDY** *leaps on* **RIZZO** *and the two girls start fighting.* **DANNY** *pulls* **SANDY** *off.*)

LET GO OF ME! YOU DIRTY LIAR! DON'T TOUCH ME!

(**SONNY** *and* **ROGER** *hold* **RIZZO**.)

RIZZO. Aaahh, let me go. I ain't gonna do nothin' to her. That chick's flipped her lid!

SANDY. *(to* **DANNY**) You tell them right now...that all those things you've been saying about me were lies. Go on, tell 'em.

DANNY. Whattaya talkin' about? I never said anything about you.

SANDY. You creep! You think you're such a big man, don't ya? Trying to make me look like just another tramp.

(**RIZZO** *charges at her. The guys hold* **RIZZO** *back.*)

I don't know *why* I ever liked you, Danny Zuko.

(**SANDY** *runs off in tears, stepping on* **FRENCHY**'*s fan magazine.* **DANNY** *starts after her…gives up.* **FRENCHY** *sadly picks up torn Rick Nelson picture.*)

DANNY. *(turning to the others)* Weird chick! *(pause)* Hey, Rizzo. You wanna go to the dance with me?

RIZZO. Huh? Yeah, sure. Why not?

ROGER. Hey,

JAN. You got a date for the dance tomorrow night?

JAN. Tomorrow? Let me see – *(She takes out a little notebook and thumbs through it.)* No, I don't. Why?

ROGER. You wanna go with me?

JAN. You kiddin' me?

(**ROGER** *shakes his head "no."*)

Yeah, sure, Roge!

DOODY. *(very shy, moving to* **FRENCHY***)* Hey, Frenchy, can you still go to the dance, now that you quit school?

FRENCHY. Yeah. I guess so. Why?

DOODY. Oh… Ahh, nothin'… I'll see ya there.

SONNY. Hey, Kenickie, how 'bout givin' me a ride tomorrow, and I'll pick us up a couple ah broads at the dance.

DANNY. With what? A meat hook?

KENICKIE. Nah, I got a blind date from 'cross town. I hear she's a real bombshell.

MARTY. Gee, I don't even know if I'll go.

DANNY. Why not, Marty?

MARTY. I ain't got a date.

DANNY. Hey, I know just the guy. *(Pause. Yells offstage.)* Hey, Eugene!

(**MARTY** *starts to chase* **DANNY** *hitting him with magazine.*)

[MUSIC NO. 10: WE GO TOGETHER]

ALL.

WE GO TOGETHER, LIKE A
RAMA-LAMA-LAMA, KA-DINGITY DING-DE-DONG
REMEMBERED FOREVER, AS
SHOO-BOP SHA WADDA WADDA
YIPPITY BOOM-DE-BOOM
CHANG CHANG CHANGITTY-CHANG SHOO BOP
THAT'S THE WAY IT SHOULD BE (WHAA-OOHH! YEAH!)

WE'RE ONE OF A KIND, LIKE
DIP-DA-DIP-DA-DIP
DOO WOP DA DOOBY DOO
OUR NAMES ARE SIGNED
BOOGEDY, BOOGEDY, BOOGEDY, BOOGEDY, SHOOBY-DOO
    WOP-SHA-BOP
CHANG CHANG CHANGITY CHANG SHOO BOP
WE'LL ALWAYS BE LIKE ONE (WHAA-WHA-WHA- WHA-OOH)

WHEN WE GO OUT AT NIGHT
AND STARS ARE SHINING BRIGHT
UP IN THE SKIES ABOVE
OR AT THE HIGH SCHOOL DANCE
WHERE YOU CAN FIND ROMANCE
MAYBE IT MIGHT BE LA-A-A-AH-OVE!

ROGER & JAN.

RAMA LAMA LAMA KA-DINGITY DING-DE-DONG

MARTY & KENICKIE.

SHOO BOP SHA WADDA, WADDA YIPPYDI BOOM-DE-BOOM

FRENCHY & DOODY.

CHANG CHANG, CHANGITY CHANG SHOO BOP

SONNY.

DIP DA DIP DA DIP DOO BOP DA DOO-BE DOO

DANNY & RIZZO.

BOOGEDY, BOOGEDY, BOOGEDY, BOOGEDY, SHOOBY DOO
    WOP SHA BOP

ALL.

> SHANA-NA-NA-NA-NA-NA-NA YIPPIDY DIP DE DOO
> RAMA LAMA LAMA KA-DINGITY DING DE-DONG
> SHOO BOP SHA WADDA WADDA YIPPY-DI BOOM-DE-BOOM
> CHANG CHANG CHANGITY CHANG SHOO BOP
> DIP DA DIP DA DIP DOO BOP DA DOOBE DOO.
> BOOGEDY BOOGEDY BOOGEDY BOOGEDY BOOGEDY
>   SHOOBY DOO WOP SHA BOP
> SHANA-NA-NA-NA-NA-NA-NA YIPPIDY DIP DE DOO

DANNY.

> A WOP BAM-A-LU MOP AND WOP BAM BOOM

ALL.

> WE'RE FOR EACH OTHER, LIKE
> A WOP BAB A LU MOP AHH WOP BAM BOOM!
> JUST LIKE MY BROTHER, IS
> SHA NA NA NA NA NA YIPPITY DIP DE DOOM
> CHANG CHANG-A CHANGITY CHANG SHOO BOP
> WE'LL ALWAYS BE TOGETHER. WOH-OH YEAH!

GIRLS.

> ALWAYS BE TOGETHER.

BOYS.

> CHANG CHANG CHANGITY CHANG SHOO BOP
> CHANG CHANG CHANGITY CHANG SHOO BOP

GIRLS.

> ALWAYS BE TOGETHER.

BOYS.

> CHANG CHANG CHANGITY CHANG SHOO BOP
> CHANG CHANG CHANGITY CHANG SHOO BOP

GIRLS.

> ALWAYS BE TOGETHER.

BOYS.

> CHANG CHANG CHANGITY CHANG SHOO BOP
> CHANG CHANG CHANGITY CHANG SHOO BOP

> *(At the end of the song, the lights fade on the kids as they go off laughing and horsing around.)*

End of Act One

ACT TWO

Scene One

*(Scene: The **GREASERS** run on and sing "Shakin' at the High School Hop." They are preparing for the high school dance – the boys combing hair, polishing shoes, etc. – the girls spraying hair, putting on crinolines, stuffing Kleenex into bras, etc.)*

[MUSIC NO. 11: SHAKIN' AT THE HIGH SCHOOL HOP]

ALL.

> WELL, HONKY-TONK BABY, GET ON THE FLOOR
> ALL THE CATS ARE SHOUTIN', THEY'RE YELLIN' FOR MORE
> MY BABY LIKES TO ROCK, MY BABY LIKES TO ROLL
> MY BABY DOES THE CHICKEN AND SHE DOES THE STROLL:
> WELL, SHAKE IT
> OHH, SHAKE IT
> YEAH, SHAKE IT
> EVERYBODY SHAKIN'
> SHAKIN' AT THE HIGH SCHOOL HOP

DANNY.

> WELL, SOCK-HOP BABY,

GIRLS.

> ROLL UP YOUR CRAZY JEANS

GUYS.

> GONNA ROCK TO THE MUSIC,

ALL.

> GONNA DIG THE SCENE

GIRLS.

> SHIMMY TO THE LEFT,

ALL.

> A-CHA-CHA TO THE RIGHT
> WE GONNA DO THE WALK 'TIL BROAD DAYLIGHT
> WELL, SHAKE IT
> YEAH, SHAKE IT
> YEAH, SHAKE IT
> EVERYBODY SHAKIN'
> SHAKIN' AT THE HIGH SCHOOL HOP

GIRLS.

> WE'RE GONNA ALLEY-OOP ON BLUEBERRY HILL

GUYS.

> HULLY-GULLY WITH LUCILLE, WON'T BE STANDIN' STILL

ALL.

> HAND-JIVE BABY
> DO THE STOMP WITH ME
> I CHA-LYPSO, DO THE SLOP GONNA BOP WITH MR. LEE
>
> WELL, THEY SHAKE IT
> SHAKE, ROCK AND ROLL
> ROCK, ROLL AND SHAKE
> SHAKE, ROCK AND ROLL
> ROCK, ROLL AND SHAKE
> SHAKE, ROCK AND ROLL

> *(Instrumental chorus and dance. During instrumental section, the* **GREASERS** *move into the High School gym and are joined by* **PATTY, EUGENE** *and* **MISS LYNCH, ALL** *dancing wildly.)*

> SHAKE, ROCK AND ROLL
> ROCK, ROLL AND SHAKE
> SHAKE, ROCK AND ROLL
> ROCK, ROLL AND SHAKE
> SHAKE, ROCK AND ROLL

> *(Lights fade on dance and* **SANDY** *is revealed in her bedroom. She turns up the volume on radio.)*

ANNOUNCER. ...Continuing lovely dreamtime music on WLDL with a popular success from last summer: "It's Raining on Prom Night"...

(Song comes on radio. **SANDY** *sings lead vocal with the radio voice in harmony.)*

[MUSIC NO. 12: IT'S RAINING ON PROM NIGHT]

RADIO VOICE.

I WAS DEPRIVED OF A YOUNG GIRL'S DREAM
BY THE CRUEL FORCE OF NATURE FROM THE BLUE

SANDY & RADIO VOICE.

INSTEAD OF A NIGHT FULL OF ROMANCE SUPREME
ALL I GOT WAS A RUNNY NOSE AND ASIATIC FLU

IT'S RAINING ON PROM NIGHT
MY HAIR IS A MESS
IT'S RUNNING ALL OVER
MY TAFFETA DRESS
IT'S WILTING THE QUILTING IN MY MAIDENFORM
AND MASCARA FLOWS, RIGHT DOWN MY NOSE BECAUSE OF
     THE STORM
I DON'T EVEN HAVE MY CORSAGE, OH GEE
IT FELL DOWN A SEWER WITH MY SISTER'S I.D.

*(***SANDY*** talks verse while* **RADIO VOICE** *continues to sing.)*

YES, IT'S RAINING ON PROM NIGHT
OH, WHAT CAN I DO? I MISS YOU
IT'S RAINING RAIN FROM THE SKIES
IT'S RAINING REAL TEARS FROM MY EYES
OVER YOU.

Dear God, let him feel the same way I do right now.
Make him want to see me again! *(***SANDY*** resumes singing the lead.)*

IT'S RAINING ON PROM NIGHT
OH, WHAT CAN I DO?
IT'S RAINING RAIN FROM THE SKIES
IT'S RAINING TEARS FROM MY EYES
OVER YOU – OOO-OOO-OOO-RAIN-ING.

[MUSIC NO. 12A: SCENE CHANGE INTO HIGH SCHOOL HOP]

(After song, "Shakin' at the High School Hop" continues. Lights fade out on SANDY, come up on the high school dance. The couples are: DANNY and RIZZO, JAN and ROGER, FRENCHY and DOODY. MISS LYNCH is overseeing the punchbowl. MARTY is alone and SONNY is drinking from a half-pint in the corner. At the end of "Shakin'" the kids cheer and yell. JOHNNY CASINO, with guitar on bandstand, introduces VINCE FONTAINE, announcer for radio station WAXX.)

JOHNNY CASINO. Hang loose, everybody – here he is, the Main Brain – Vince Fontaine.

(VINCE FONTAINE dashes on and grabs mike.)

VINCE. I've had a lot of requests for a slow one. How 'bout it, Johnny Casino?

JOHNNY CASINO. *(grabbing mike)* Okay, Vince, here's a little number I wrote called "Enchanted Guitar."

VINCE. *(grabbing mike back)* And don't forget, only ten more minutes 'til the big Hand-Jive Contest.

(cheers and excited murmurs from the crowd)

So, if you've got a steady get her ready.

[MUSIC NO. 12B: UNDERSCORE INTO HIGH SCHOOL HOP]

(JOHNNY CASINO and the BAND do slow two-step instrumental as VINCE leaves bandstand and mills among kids.)

RIZZO. Hey, Danny, you gonna be my partner for the dance contest?

DANNY. Maybe, if nothing better comes along.

RIZZO. Drop dead!

JAN. *(stumbling on ROGER's feet)* Sorry.

ROGERS. Why don'tcha let *me* lead, for a change?

JAN. I can't help it. I'm used to leading.

FRENCHY. *(dancing with* DOODY, *who is rocking back and forth in one spot)* Hey, Doody, can't you at least turn me around or somethin'?

DOODY. Don't talk, I'm tryin' to count.

(PATTY dances near DANNY with EUGENE, who is pumping her arm vigorously.)

PATTY. Danny, Danny!

DANNY. Yeah, that's my name, don't wear it out.

PATTY. How did the track tryouts go?

DANNY. *(nonchalantly)* I made the team.

PATTY. Oh, wonderful! *(PATTY starts signaling in pantomime for DANNY to cut in.)*

RIZZO. Hey, Zuko, I think she's tryin' to tell ya somethin'!

(PATTY's pantomime becomes more desperate as EUGENE pumps harder.)

Go on, dance with her. You ain't doin' me no good.

DANNY. *(going up to EUGENE)* Hey, Euuu-gene, Betty Rizzo thinks you look like Pat Boone.

EUGENE. Oh?

(EUGENE walks over and stands near RIZZO, staring. He polishes his white bucks on the backs of his pant legs. DANNY dances with PATTY.)

RIZZO. Whataya say, Fruit Boots?

EUGENE. I understand you were asking about me?

RIZZO. Yeah! I was wondering where you parked your hearse.

(EUGENE sits next to RIZZO and RIZZO offers him SONNY's half-pint. SONNY grabs it back. PATTY and DANNY in close dance clinch, not moving.)

PATTY. I never knew you were such a fabulous dancer, Danny. So sensuous and feline.

DANNY. Huh? Yeah.

(Music tempo changes to cha-cha. KENICKIE and CHA-CHA DEGREGORIO enter.)

CHA-CHA. God, nice time to get here. Look, the joint's half empty already.

KENICKIE. Ahh, knock it off! Can I help it if my car wouldn't start?

CHA-CHA. Jeez, what crummy decorations!

KENICKIE. Where'd ya think you were goin', American Bandstand?

CHA-CHA. We had a sock-hop at St. Bernadette's once. The Sisters got real pumpkins and everything.

KENICKIE. Neat. They probably didn't have a bingo game that night.

(KENICKIE walks away from her and she trails behind him.)

VINCE. *(coming up to MARTY)* Pardon me, weren't you a contestant in the Miss Rock 'N' Roll Universe Pageant?

MARTY. Yeah, but I got disqualified 'cause I had a hickey on my neck.

(The song ends and kids cheer. JOHNNY CASINO looks for VINCE FONTAINE on the dance floor.)

JOHNNY CASINO. Hey, Vince...any more requests?

VINCE. *(irritated, still looking at MARTY. Motions JOHNNY with his hand.)* Yeah, play anything!

JOHNNY CASINO. Okay, here's a little tune called "Anything"!

(Band plays instrumental "Stroll." MARTY, JAN and FRENCHY, VINCE, ROGER and DOODY form lines as DANNY and PATTY come through center.)

PATTY. I can't imagine you ever having danced with Sandy like this.

DANNY. Whattaya mean?

PATTY. I mean her being so clumsy and all. She can't even twirl a baton right. In fact, I've been thinking of having a little talk with the coach about her.

DANNY. Why? Whatta you care?

PATTY. Well, I mean...even you have to admit she's a bit of a drip. I mean...isn't that why you broke up with her?

DANNY. Hey, listen...y'know she used to be a halfway decent chick before she got mixed up with you and your brown-nose friends.

(DANNY *walks away from her.* PATTY, *stunned, runs to the punch table.* KENICKIE *walks up to* RIZZO.)

RIZZO. Hey, Kenickie, where ya been, the submarine races?

KENICKIE. Nah. I had to go to Egypt to pick up a date.

RIZZO. You feel like dancin'?

KENICKIE. Crazy.

(*He starts to dance off with* RIZZO.)

EUGENE. It's been very nice talking to you, Betty.

RIZZO. Yeah, see ya around the Bookmobile.

(CHA-CHA *moves to* EUGENE, *hoping* EUGENE *might ask her to dance, as band continues.* SONNY *gets up and crosses dance floor.*)

DOODY. (*dropping out of the stroll line*) Hey, Rump, let's go have a weed.

ROGER. Yeah, okay.

JAN. Oh, Roger, would ya get me some punch?

ROGER. Whatsa matter? You crippled?

(DOODY *and* ROGER *start off.* JAN *sticks her tongue out at* ROGER. DOODY *and* ROGER *bump into* SONNY.)

VINCE. (*doing cha-cha with* MARTY) I'm Vince Fontaine. Do your folks know I come into your room every night? Over WAXX, that is! I'm gonna judge the dance contest. Are you gonna be ink?

MARTY. I guess not. I ain't got a date.

VINCE. What? A knockout like you? Things sure have changed since I went to school...last year. Ha-Ha!

(MARTY *stares at him dumbly for a few seconds, then starts laughing.* DOODY, SONNY, ROGER *and* DANNY *are drinking and smoking in corner.* **CHA-CHA** *is dancing around* **EUGENE** *at bench.)*

DOODY. *(pointing to* **CHA-CHA**) Hey, ain't that the chick Kenickie walked in with?

SONNY. Where?

DOODY. The one pickin' her nose over there.

SONNY. That's the baby.

ROGER. Jesus, is she a gorilla!

SONNY. I thought she was one of the cafeteria ladies.

(The guys crack up.)

CHA-CHA. *(standing near* **EUGENE**) Hey, did you come here to dance or didn't ya?

EUGENE. Of course, but I never learned how to do this dance.

CHA-CHA. Ahh, there's nothing to it. I'm gonna teach "ballroom" at the CYO.

(She grabs **EUGENE** *in dance position.)*

Now, one-two-cha-cha-cha! Three-four-cha-cha-cha-very-good-cha-cha-cha-keep-it-up-cha-cha-cha...

EUGENE. You certainly dance well.

CHA-CHA. Thanks, ya can hold me a little tighter. I won't bite cha.

*(**CHA-CHA** grabs* **EUGENE** *in a bear-hug. Music ends, and kids applaud.)*

JOHNNY CASINO. Thank you. This is Johnny Casino telling you when you hear the tone it will be exactly one minute to "Hand-Jive" time!

(Excited murmurs and scrambling for partners takes place on the dance floor as the band's guitarist makes a "twang" sound on his "E" string.)

EUGENE. *(to* **CHA-CHA**) Excuse me, it was nice meeting you.

CHA-CHA. Hey, wait a minute...don'tcha want my phone number or somethin'?

EUGENE. *(over by* PATTY*)* Patty, you promised to be my partner for the dance contest, remember?

PATTY. That's right. I almost forgot.

(She looks longingly toward DANNY *as* EUGENE *pulls her away.)*

DANNY. *(walking over to* RIZZO *and* KENICKIE*)* Hey, Rizzo. I'm ready to dance with you now.

RIZZO. Don't strain yourself... I'm dancin' with Kenickie.

KENICKIE. That's alright, Zuko, you can have my date. *(He yells.)* Hey, Charlene! Come 'ere.

CHA-CHA. *(walking over)* Yeah, whattaya want?

KENICKIE. How'dja like to dance this next one with Danny Zuko?

CHA-CHA. The big rod of the Burger Palace Boys? I didn't even know he saw me here.

DANNY. *(giving* CHA-CHA *a dismayed look)* I didn't.

*(*CHA-CHA *looks around in ecstasy.)*

JOHNNY. Okay, alligators, here it is. The big one...

(drum roll)

...the Hand-Jive Dance Contest.

(The kids cheer.)

Let's get things under way by bringing up our own Miss Lynch.

[MUSIC NO. 12C: ENTER MISS LYNCH]

(The kids react. Guitar player in band plays a few chords of "Rydell fight song" as MISS LYNCH *comes up to the mike.)*

MISS LYNCH. Thank you, Clarence.

(All the kids break up. JOHNNY CASINO *gives kids "the finger.")*

Whenever you're finished.

(Noise subsides a little.)

MISS LYNCH. Before we begin, I'd like to welcome you all to "Moonlight in the Tropics." *(Drum Hit)* And I think we all owe a big round of applause to Patty Simcox and her committee for the wonderful decorations.

(Mixed reaction from crowd.)

CHA-CHA. They shoulda got real coconuts!

MISS LYNCH. Now, I'm sure you'll be glad to know that I'm not judging this dance contest.

(A few kids cheer.)

All right. All right. I'd like to present Mr. Vince Fontaine…

(Kids cheer, as she looks around.)

…Mr. Fontaine?

[MUSIC NO. 12D: ENTER VINCE FONTAINE]

VINCE. *(Necking with* **MARTY,** *yells to* **MISS LYNCH.)** Comin' right up!

MISS LYNCH. As most of you know, Mr. Fontaine is an announcer for radio station WAXX.

*(***VINCE,*** on the bandstand, whispers in her ear.)*

…uh… *(uncomfortably)* "Dig the scene on big fifteen."

(Cheer goes up.)

Now for the rules! One: All couples must be boy-girl.

ROGER. Too bad, Eugene!

MISS LYNCH. Two: anyone using tasteless or vulgar movements will be disqualified.

RIZZO. *(loud to* **KENICKIE***)* That let's us out!

MISS LYNCH. Three: If Mr. Fontaine taps you on the shoulder, you must clear the dance floor immediately…

VINCE. *(grabbing the mike from* **MISS LYNCH***)* I just wanna say, truly in all sincerity, Miss Lynch, that you're doing a really, really terrific job here, terrific. And I'll sure bet these kids are lucky to have you for a teacher, 'cause

I'll bet in all sincerity that you're really terrific. IS SHE TERRIFIC, KIDS?

(The kids cheer.)

Only thing I wanna say, in all sincerity, is enjoy yourselves, have a ball, 'cause like we always say at "BIG FIFTEEN" where the jocks hang out – "If you're having fun, you're number one!" And some lucky guy and gal is gonna go boppin' home with a stack of terrific prizes. But don't feel bad if I bump yuzz out, 'cause it don't matter if you win or lose, it's what ya do with those dancing shoes. So, okay, cats, throw your mittens around your kittens...and AWAY WE GO!

(VINCE does a Jackie Gleason pose. JOHNNY CASINO sings "Born to Hand-Jive." During the dance, couples are eliminated one by one as VINCE FONTAINE mills through the crowd, tapping each couple and occasionally letting one of his hands slither down to rub one of the girls across the ass, or nonchalantly trying to "cop a feel")

[MUSIC NO. 13: BORN TO HAND-JIVE]

JOHNNY CASINO.

BEFORE I WAS BORN, LATE ONE NIGHT
MY PAPA SAID, EVERYTHING'S ALL RIGHT
THE DOCTOR LAUGHED, WHEN MA LAID DOWN
WITH HER STOMACH BOUNCIN' ALL AROUND
'CAUSE A BE-BOP STORK WAS 'BOUT TO ARRIVE
AND MAMA GAVE BIRTH TO THE "HAND-JIVE"!

I COULD BARELY WALK WHEN I MILKED A COW
AND WHEN I WAS THREE I PUSHED A PLOW
WHILE CHOPPIN' WOOD I'D MOVE MY LEGS
AND STARTED DANCIN' WHILE I GATHERED EGGS
THE TOWN-FOLK CLAPPED, I WAS ONLY FIVE
HE'LL OUTDANCE 'EM ALL, HE'S A BORN "HAND-JIVE"!

(Short guitar solo. Dance Chorus.)

ENSEMBLE.

> BORN TO HAND-JIVE, BABEEEEEE!
> BORN TO HAND-JIVE, BABY!
>
> *(dance)*

JOHNNY CASINO.

> SO I GREW UP DANCIN' ON THE STAGE
> DOIN' THE HAND-JIVE BECAME THE RAGE
> BUT A JEALOUS STUD PULLED A GUN   *optional*
> AND SAID "LET'S SEE HOW FAST YOU RUN?"   *Verse*
> YEAH, NATURAL RHYTHM KEPT ME ALIVE
> OUT-DODGIN' BULLETS WITH THE OL' HAND-JIVE!
>
> NOW, CAN YOU HAND-JIVE, BABEEEEEEE?
> OH, CAN YOU HAND-JIVE, BABY?
> BORN TO HAND-JIVE, BABY!
> BORN TO HAND-JIVE, BABY!
> OH, YEAH, OH, YEAH, OH, YEAH. BORN TO HAND-JIVE!

(Eventually, all the couples are eliminated except **DANNY** *and* **CHA-CHA.** *On the final chorus, the kids stand around in a half circle and clap in time.* **VINCE FONTAINE** *pulls* **MISS LYNCH** *onto the dance floor and tries to hog the spotlight from* **DANNY** *and* **CHA-CHA.** *At the end of the dance,* **MISS LYNCH,** *out of breath, returns to the bandstand,* **VINCE FONTAINE** *right behind her.)*

MISS LYNCH. My goodness! Well, we have our winners. Will you step up here for your prizes? Daniel Zuko and... and...

*(***DANNY*** and ***CHA-CHA,*** swamped by the other kids, battle their way to the bandstand.)*

CHA-CHA. Cha-Cha DiGregorio.

MISS LYNCH. *(taken aback at having to repeat the first name)* Uh... Cha-Cha DiGregorio.

CHA-CHA. *(grabbing mike)* They call me Cha-Cha 'cause I'm the best dancer at St. Bernadette's.

(mixed reaction and ad-libs from crowd)

MISS LYNCH. Oh…that's very nice. Congratulations to both of you, and here are your prizes: two record albums. "Hits from the House of WAXX" autographed by Mr. Vince Fontaine.

(She holds up album with large letters: WAXX. Kids cheer.)

Two free passes to the Twi-Light Drive In Theatre… good on any week night.

(Kids cheer.)

A coupon worth ten dollars off at Robert Hall.

(Kids boo.)

And last but not least, your trophies, prepared by Mrs. Schneider's art class.

*(Cheers and applause. **MISS LYNCH** presents **DANNY** and **CHA-CHA** with two hideous ceramic nebbishes in dance positions, mounted on blocks of wood.)*

VINCE. *(grabbing the mike from **MISS LYNCH**)* Weren't they terrific? C'mon, let's hear it for these kids! *(Kids cheer.)* Only thing I wanna say before we wrap things up is that you kids at Rydell are the greatest!

KENICKIE. Friggin'A!

VINCE. Last dance, ladies' choice.

*(Band plays slow instrumental. **DANNY** takes record album from **CHA-CHA**, in exchange giving her his trophy and he exits. Couples leave dance, one by one until **CHA-CHA** is left alone, as **PATTY**, **EUGENE** and **MISS LYNCH** clean after dance. Each exits, as the lights change to new scene.)*

[MUSIC NO. 13A: CROSSOVER ("LAST DANCE") OUT OF HOP]

Scene Two

(Scene: It is evening a few days later in front of the Burger Palace. **FRENCHY** *is pacing around, magazine in hand, looking at a sign on the Burger Palace window: "Counter Girl Wanted." After a few moments* **SONNY**, **KENICKIE,** *and* **DOODY** *enter with weapons:* **DOODY** *with a baseball bat,* **SONNY** *with a zip-gun,* **KENICKIE** *with a lead pipe and chain. They wear leather jackets and engineer boots.)*

KENICKIE. Hey, Sonny, what cracker-jack box 'ja get that zip gun out of, anyway?

SONNY. What do ya mean, I made it in shop. *(seeing* **FRENCHY***)* Hey, what's shakin', French? You get out of Beauty School already?

FRENCHY. Oh… I cut tonight. Those beauty teachers they got working there don't know nothin'. Hey, what's with the arsenal?

DOODY. We gotta rumble with the Flaming Dukes.

FRENCHY. No lie! How come?

KENICKIE. Remember that grungey broad I took to the dance?

*(***FRENCHY** *looks blank.)*

DOODY. *(helpfully)* Godzilla!

*(***DOODY** *and* **KENICKIE** *do imitation of* **CHA-CHA** *and* **EUGENE** *dancing. While* **KENICKIE** *imitates picking his nose.)*

DOODY & KENICKIE. "One-two – cha-cha-cha!"

FRENCHY. Oh! Y'mean Cha-Cha Dee Garage-io…the one Danny won the dance contest with?

SONNY. Well, it turns out she goes steady with the leader of the Flaming Dukes. And, she told this guy Danny tried to put his hands all over her.

KENICKIE. If he did, he musta been makin' a bug collection for Biology.

(All guys laugh, **KENICKIE** *joins in laughing at his own joke.* **DANNY** *enters jogging, wearing a white track suit with a brown and green number "4" on his back. The trunks are white with a thin green and brown stripe running vertically on each side. He has a relay-race baton.)*

FRENCHY. *(Seeing* **DANNY.***)* Hey look…ain't that Danny?

DOODY. Hey, Danny!

FRENCHY. What's he doing in his underwear?

DOODY. That's a track suit! Hi ya, Danny.

*(***DANNY*** stops. He's panting. Guys gather around him.)*

KENICKIE. Jesus, Zuko, where do you keep your "Wheaties?"

DANNY. *(reaching in front of jock strap and pulling out a crumpled pack of Luckies)* Ha-ha. Big joke. *(***DANNY*** lights a cigarette and holds pack in his hand.)*

SONNY. Hey, it's a good thing you're here. We're supposed to rumble the Dukes tonight!

DANNY. *(alarmed)* What time?

KENICKIE. Nine o'clock.

DANNY. *(annoyed)* Nice play! I got field training till nine-thirty.

KENICKIE. Can't ya sneak away, man?

DANNY. Not a chance! The coach'd kick my butt.

SONNY. The coach!

DANNY. Besides, what am I supposed to do, stomp on somebody's face with my gym shoes? *(He puts cigarettes back in jock.)*

KENICKIE. Ahh, c'mon, Zuko, whattaya tryin' to prove with this track team crap?!

DANNY. Why? Whatta you care? Look, I gotta cut. I'm in the middle of a race now. See ya' later. *(***DANNY*** starts off.)*

SONNY. You got "the hots" for that cheerleader or somethin'?

DANNY. *(runs back angry)* How'd you like a fat lip, Sonny?

SONNY. Zuko, we're gonna get creamed without you.

DANNY. Nine o'clock, huh? I'll be back if I can get away. Later! *(Silence,* **DANNY** *stands glaring at the guys for a moment and then he runs off, cigarette in his mouth.)*

SONNY. Neat guy, causes a ruckus and then he cuts out on us!

KENICKIE. Jeez, next thing ya know he'll be gettin' a crew-cut!

DOODY. He'd look neater with a flat top.

KENICKIE. C'mon, let's go eat.

(He and **SONNY** *start towards Burger Palace.)*

SONNY. Hey, Knicks, you wanna split a super-buger?

KENICKIE. Yeah. All right.

SONNY. Good. Lend me a half a buck.

*(***SONNY** *and* **KENICKIE** *exit into Burger Palace stashing their weapons in a painted oil drum used for garbage.)*

DOODY. Hey, Frenchy, maybe I'll come down to your beauty school some night this week...we can have a Coke or somethin'.

FRENCHY. *(uncertain)* Yeah...yeah, sure.

*(***DOODY** *smiles and, depositing his baseball bat in the same oil can, exits into the Burger Palace. To her movie magazine.)*

Jeez! What am I gonna do? I mean, I can't just tell everybody I dropped out of beauty school. I can't go in the Palace for a job...with all the guys sittin' around. Boy, I wish I had one of those Guardian Angel things like in that Debbie Reynolds movie. Would that be neat...somebody always there to tell ya' what's the best thing to do.

(Spooky angelic guitar chords. **FRENCHY***'s guardian* **TEEN ANGEL** *appears swinging in quietly on a rope. He is a Fabian-like rock singer. White Fabian sweater with the collar turned up, white chinos, white boots, a large white comb sticking out of his pocket. He sings* "BEAUTY SCHOOL DROPOUT." *After the first verse,*

a chorus of **ANGELS** *appears: a group of* **GIRLS** *in white plastic sheets and their hair in white plastic rollers in a halo effect. They provide background Doo-wahs. The* **TEEN ANGEL** *sings.)*

[MUSIC NO. 14: BEAUTY SCHOOL DROPOUT]

TEEN ANGEL.

> YOUR STORY'S SAD TO TELL
> A TEENAGE NE'ER-DO-WELL
> MOST MIXED-UP NON-DELINQUENT ON THE BLOCK
> YOUR FUTURE'S SO UNCLEAR NOW
> WHAT'S LEFT OF YOUR CAREER NOW
> CAN'T EVEN GET A TRADE-IN ON YOUR SMOCK.

> *(GIRLS enter, dressed in plastic beautician's robes and curlers. They sing "Ya, ya" backup throughout.)*

> BEAUTY SCHOOL DROPOUT
> NO GRADUATION DAY FOR YOU
> BEAUTY SCHOOL DROPOUT
> MISSED YOUR MID-TERMS AND FLUNKED SHAMPOO
> WELL, AT LEAST YOU COULD HAVE TAKEN TIME
> TO WASH AND CLEAN YOUR CLOTHES UP
> AFTER SPENDING ALL THAT DOUGH TO HAVE
> THE DOCTOR FIX YOUR NOSE UP

> BABY, GET MOVIN'
> WHY KEEP YOUR FEEBLE HOPES ALIVE?
> WHAT ARE YOU PROVIN'?
> YOU GOT THE DREAM BUT NOT THE DRIVE
> IF YOU GO FOR YOUR DIPLOMA YOU COULD JOIN A STENO
>   POOL
> TURN IN YOUR TEASING COMB AND GO BACK TO HIGH
>   SCHOOL.

> BEAUTY SCHOOL DROPOUT
> HANGIN' AROUND THE CORNER STORE
> BEAUTY SCHOOL DROPOUT
> IT'S ABOUT TIME YOU KNEW THE SCORE
> WELL, THEY COULDN'T TEACH YOU ANYTHING
> YOU THINK YOU'RE SUCH A LOOKER

BUT NO CUSTOMER WOULD GO TO YOU
UNLESS SHE WAS A HOOKER.

BABY, DON'T SWEAT IT
YOU'RE NOT CUT OUT TO HOLD A JOB
BETTER FORGET IT
WHO WANTS THEIR HAIR DONE BY A SLOB?
NOW YOUR BANGS ARE CURLED, YOUR LASHES TWIRLED,
BUT STILL THE WORLD IS CRUEL
WIPE OFF THAT ANGEL FACE AND GO BACK TO HIGH
    SCHOOL.

(At the end of the song the **TEEN ANGEL** *hands* **FRENCHY** *a high school diploma, which she uncurls, looks at, crumples up, and throws away. The* **TEEN ANGEL** *and* **CHOIR** *look on.* **FRENCHY** *walks away.)*

[MUSIC NO. 14A: BEAUTY SCHOOL DROP OUT REPRISE]

TEEN ANGEL.

BABY, YA BLEW IT
YOU PUT OUR GOOD ADVICE TO SHAME
HOW COULD YOU DO IT?
BETCHA DEAR ABBY'D SAY THE SAME.
GUESS THERE'S NO WAY TO GET THROUGH TO YOU
NO MATTER WHO MAY TRY
MIGHT AS WELL GO BACK TO THAT MALT SHOP
IN THE SKY.
YAH.

*(***CHOIR*** exits and* **TEEN ANGEL** *swings off on rope.* **FRENCHY** *exits.* **DOODY, KENICKIE,** *and* **SONNY** *come out of Burger Palace as the place is closing. The* **GUYS** *retrieve their weapons from the trash can.)*

SONNY. Looks like they ain't gonna show. They said they'd be here at nine.

DOODY. What time is it?

SONNY. *(looking at his watch)* Hey man, it's almost five after... C'mon, let's split.

KENICKIE. Give 'em another ten minutes. Hey, what the hell happened to Rump?

SONNY. Who cares about Dumbo. Who'da ever thought Zuko'd punk out on us.

KENICKIE. Nice rumble! A herd of Flaming Dukes against you, me, and Howdy Doody.

DOODY. Hey, I heard about this one time when the Dukes pulled a sneak attack by drivin' up in a stolen laundry truck. That really musta been cool.

SONNY. *(suddenly)* Hey, you guys, watch out for a cruisin' laundry truck.

(**SONNY** *and* **KENICKIE** *tense up looking around –* **DOODY** *stares blankly.* **ROGER** *comes charging on in a frenzy, with a car antenna in his hand and shouting.)*

ROGER. Okay, where the hell are they? Lemme at 'em! *(looking around)* Hey, where's Zuko?

SONNY. Well, look who's here. Where you been, meat ball?

ROGER. Hey, bite the weenie, moron. My old man made me help him paint the damned basement. I couldn't even find my bullwhip. I had to bust off an aerial.

SONNY. Ha, whattaya expect to do with that thing?

KENICKIE. *(grabbing* **ROGER**'s *antenna and imitating a newscaster)* This is Dennis James bringing you the play-by-play of Championship Gangfighting!

ROGER. *(grabbing antenna back)* Hey, listen, I'll take this over any of *those* tinker toys!

KENICKIE. Oh, yeah? Okay, Rump, how 'bout if I hit ya over the head with that thing and then I hit ya over the head with my lead pipe and you can tell me which one hurts more – okay?

ROGER. Okay. C'mon and get it! C'mon, Kenickie!

(He holds out the antenna. As **KENICKIE** *reaches for it he lashes the air above* **KENICKIE**'s *head and almost hits* **SONNY** *behind him.)*

SONNY. Hey, watch it with that thing, Pimple Puss!

ROGER. Hey, whatsa matter, LaTierri, afraid ya might get hurt a little?

SONNY. Listen, Chicken Fat, you're gonna look real funny cruisin' around the neighborhood in an iron lung.

ROGER. Well, why don'tcha use that thing, then? You got enough rubber bands there to start three paper routes.

KENICKIE. *(grabbing* **DOODY***'s baseball bat)* Hey. Rump! C'mon, let's see ya try that again.

ROGER. What'sa matter, Kenicks? What happened to your big bad pipe?

*(***SONNY***,* ***DOODY***,* ***KENICKIE***, and* ***ROGER*** *begin circling.* ***KENICKIE*** *knocks antenna out of* ***ROGER***'s hand with bat.* ***KENICKIE*** *and* ***SONNY*** *close in on* ***ROGER***, now defenseless.)*

KENICKIE. Okay, Rump, how's about mooning the Flaming Dukes? Pants 'im!

*(***SONNY*** *and* ***KENICKIE*** *leap on* ***ROGER*** *and get his pants off.* ***DOODY*** *helps with the shoes.* ***SONNY*** *and* ***KENICKIE*** *run off with* ***ROGER***'s pants as ***DOODY*** *gathers up weapons.)*

DOODY. Hey, you guys, wait up!

*(***DOODY*** *starts to run off, then goes back to hand* ***ROGER*** *his antenna.* ***DOODY*** *exits.)*

ROGER. Oh, crap!

*(***ROGER*** *stands a moment bewildered, holding antenna and his shoes, then exits disgusted.)*

[MUSIC NO. 14B: SCENE CHANGE INTO DRIVE IN MOVIE]

Scene Three

(Scene: Scene comes up on Greased Lightning at the Twi-Light Drive-In Theatre. **SANDY** *and* **DANNY** *are sitting alone at opposite ends of the front seat staring straight ahead in awkward silence. Movie music is coming out of a portable speaker.* **DANNY** *is sipping a quart of beer. Dialogue from the movie begins to come out of the speaker over eerie background music.)*

GIRL'S VOICE. It was…like an animal…with awful clawing hands and…and…hideous fangs…oh, it was like a nightmare!

HERO'S VOICE. There, there, you're safe now, Sheila.

SCIENTIST'S VOICE. Poor Todd. The radiation has caused him to mutate. He's become half-man, half-monster… like a werewolf.

SHEILA'S VOICE. But, doctor…he…he's my *brother.* And his big stock car race is tomorrow!

(A werewolf cry is heard.)

HERO'S VOICE. Great Scott! It's a full moon!

(Silence. **DANNY** *stretches, puts arm across* **SANDY**'s *shoulder.* **DANNY** *tries to get arm around her. She moves away.)*

DANNY. Why don'tcha move over a little closer? *(removes arm from across the back of seat)*

SANDY. This is all right.

DANNY. Well, can't ya at least smile or somethin'? Look, Sandy, I practically had to bust Kenickie's arm to get his car for tonight. The guys are really P.O.'d at me. I mean, I thought we were gonna forget all about that scene in the park with Sonny and Rizzo and everything. I told ya on the phone I was sorry.

SANDY. I know you did.

DANNY. Well, you believe me, don't ya?

SANDY. I guess so. It's just that everything was so much easier when there was just the two of us.

DANNY. Yeah, I know…but… *(suddenly)* Hey, you ain't goin' with another guy, are ya?

SANDY. No. Why?

DANNY. *(taking off his high school ring)* Err…oh, ah… nothin'…well, yeah…uh…ahhh, *(has trouble removing ring – runs ring through hair and it comes off)* I was gonna ask ya to take my ring. *(He holds out the ring.)*

SANDY. Oh, Danny… I don't know what to say.

DANNY. Well, don'tcha want it?

SANDY. *(smiles shyly)* Uh-huh.

> *(DANNY puts ring on SANDY's finger. She kisses him lightly.)*

DANNY. I shoulda gave it to ya' a long time ago.

> *(They kiss.)*

I really like you, Sandy.

> *(They kiss again. DANNY getting more aggressive and passionate as the kiss goes on.)*

SANDY. Danny, take it easy! What are you trying to do? *(SANDY squirms away from him.)*

DANNY. What'sa matter?

SANDY. Well, I mean… I thought we were just gonna – you know – be steadies.

DANNY. Well, whattaya think goin' steady is, anyway?

> *(He grabs her again.)*

C'mon, Sandy!

SANDY. Stop it! I've never seen you like this.

DANNY. Relax, will ya, nobody's watchin' us!

SANDY. Danny, please, you're hurting me.

> *(DANNY lets go and SANDY breaks away.)*

DANNY. Whattaya gettin' so shook up about? I thought I meant somethin' to ya.

SANDY. You do. But I'm still the same girl I was last summer. Just because you give me your ring doesn't mean we're gonna go all the way.

(**SANDY** *opens the car door, gets out.*)

DANNY. Hey, Sandy, wait a minute.

(**SANDY** *slams car door on* **DANNY**'s *hand.*)

SANDY. I'm sorry, Danny…

DANNY. *(in pain, falsetto voice)* It's nothing!

SANDY. Maybe we better just forget about it.

(**SANDY** *gives* **DANNY** *his ring back. When he refuses, she leaves it on car hood. She exits.*)

DANNY. *(yelling)* Hey, Sandy, where you goin? You can't just walk out of a drive-in!

(*Movie voices are heard again.*)

HERO'S VOICE. Look, Sheila! The full moon is sinking behind "Dead Man's Curve."

(**DANNY** *gets out of car to get ring.*)

SHEILA'S VOICE. Yes, Lance…and with it…all our dreams.

(*Werewolf howl.* **DANNY** *sings "Alone At The Drive-In Movie" with werewolf howls coming from movie and the* **BURGER PALACE BOYS** *singing background doo-wops in* **DANNY**'s *mind offstage.*)

[MUSIC NO. 15: ALONE AT THE DRIVE IN MOVIE]

DANNY.

I'M ALL ALONE
AT THE DRIVE-IN MOVIE
IT'S A FEELIN' THAT AINT TOO GROOVY
WATCHING WEREWOLVES WITHOUT YOU.

(offstage wolf howl)

GEE, IT'S NO FUN
DRINKIN' BEER IN THE BACK SEAT

ALL ALONE JUST AINT TOO NEAT
AT THE PASSION PIT, WANTING YOU.

SONNY.

DOW DOW DOW DOW DOW DOW DOW

DANNY.

AND WHEN THE INTERMISSION ELF

(**DANNY**, **ROGER**, **KENICKIE**, *and* **SONNY** *sing backup throughout.*)

MOVES THE CLOCK'S HANDS
WHILE HE'S EATING EVERYTHING
SOLD AT THE STAND

(**DANNY** *gets into car.*)

WHEN THERE'S ONE MINUTE TO GO
TILL THE LIGHTS GO DOWN LOW
I'LL BE HOLDING THE SPEAKER KNOBS
MISSING YOU SO.

CAN'T BELIEVE IT
UNSTEAMED WINDOWS I CAN SEE THROUGH
MIGHT AS WELL BE IN AN IGLOO
'CAUSE THE HEATER DOESN'T WORK...
AS GOOD AS YOU.

(*Lights fade on* **DANNY** *after song as he drives off in car.*)

Scene Four

*(Scene: A party in **JAN**'s basement. **ROGER** and **DOODY** sitting on barstools singing "Rock 'N' Roll Party Queen" accompanied by **DOODY**'s guitar. **KENICKIE** and **RIZZO** are dancing. **SONNY** and **MARTY** are on couch tapping feet and drinking beer. **FRENCHY** is sitting on floor next to record player keeping time to the music. **JAN** is swaying to the music. **SANDY** sits alone on stairs trying to fit in and enjoy herself. **DANNY** is not present.)*

[MUSIC NO. 16: ROCK 'N' ROLL PARTY QUEEN]

DOODY & ROGER.
LITTLE GIRL – D'YA KNOW WHO I MEAN
PRETTY SOON SHE'LL BE SEVENTEEN
THEY TELL ME HER NAME'S BETTY JEAN
HA – HA – HA ROCK 'N' ROLL PARTY QUEEN

FRIDAY NIGHT AND SHE'S GOT A DATE
GOIN' PLACES – JUSTA STAYIN' OUT LATE
DROPPIN' DIMES IN THE RECORD MACHINE
AH-HO-HO, ROCK 'N' ROLL PARTY QUEEN.

PA-PA-PA-PA-PA, OH, NO
CAN I HAVE THE CAR TONIGHT?
BAY-BA BAY-BEE, CAN I BE THE ONE
TO LOVE YOU WITH ALL MY MIGHT (I-YI-YI-YI)

SHE'S THE GIRL – THAT ALL THE KIDS KNOW
TALK ABOUT HER WHEREVER SHE GO-OH
I COULD WRITE A FAN MAGAZINE
ABOUT MY ROCK 'N' ROLL PARTY QUEEN.

BOMP-BA – BOMP-BA-BOMP, YOU SHOULD SEE
HER SHAKE TO THE LATEST DANCE
BAY-BA BAY-BEE NO, DON'T CALL IT PUPPY LOVE
DON'T YOU WANT A TRUE ROMANCE? (I-YI-YI-YI)

ROCKIN' AND A ROLLIN' LITTLE PARTY QUEEN
WE'RE GONNA DO THE STROLL, HEY PARTY QUEEN
YOU KNOW I LOVE YOU SO, MY PARTY QUEEN
YOU'RE MY ROCKIN' AND MY ROLLIN'...
PARTY QUEE-EEN!

SANDY. Don't put too many records on, Frenchy. I'm going to leave in a couple of minutes.

KENICKIE. Aahh, come on! You ain't takin' your record player already! The party's just gettin' started.

RIZZO. *(moving to* **SANDY** *at steps.)* Yeah, she's cuttin' out 'cause Zuko ain't here.

SANDY. No, I'm not! I didn't come here to see him.

RIZZO. No? What'dja come for, then?

SANDY. Uh…because I was invited.

RIZZO. We only invited ya 'cause we needed a record player.

JAN. *(Trying to avoid trouble, she motions to* **FRENCHY** *to come out to the kitchen.)* Hey, French!

FRENCHY. *(Coming over to* **SANDY** *and putting her hand on* **SANDY**'s *arm.)* Don't mind her, Sandy. C'mon, let's go help Jan fix the food.

(The guys all gather together at the couch looking at a View Master.)

MARTY. *(moving to* **RIZZO**, *who is sitting alone on steps)* Jesus, you're really a barrel of laughs tonight, Rizzo… You havin' your friend?

RIZZO. Huh?

MARTY. Your friend. Your period.

RIZZO. Don't I wish! I'm about five days late.

MARTY. You think maybe you're p.g.?

RIZZO. I don't know – big deal.

MARTY. How'd you let a thing like that happen anyway?

RIZZO. It wasn't my fault. The guy was usin' a thing, but it broke.

MARTY. Holy cow!

RIZZO. Yeah. He got it in a machine at a gas station. Y'know, one of those four-for-a-quarter jobs.

MARTY. Jeez, what a cheapskate!

*(**KENICKE** gets can of beer; near **MARTY** and **RIZZO**.)*

Hey, it's not Kenickie, is it?

RIZZO. Nah! You don't know the guy.

MARTY. Aahh, they're all the same! Ya remember that disc jockey I met at the dance. I caught him puttin' aspirin in my Coke.

RIZZO. Hey, promise you won't tell anybody, huh?

MARTY. Sure, I won't say nothin'.

RIZZO. *(moves to guys at couch)* Hey, what happened to the music? Why don't you guys sing another song?

ROGER. Okay. Hey, Dude, let's do that new one by the Tinkle-tones?

(JAN, FRENCHY and SANDY come on to hear song.)

DOODY & ROGER. *(sing)*
EACH NIGHT I CRY MYSELF TO SLEEP
THE GIRL I LOVE IS GONE FOR KEEPS...
OOO-WA OOO-OOO-WA...

(During the start of song, MARTY whispers to KENICKIE, who angrily goes over to RIZZO.)

KENICKIE. *(loud)* Hey, Rizzo, I hear you're knocked up.

(Song stops.)

RIZZO. *(glaring at MARTY)* You do, huh? Boy, good news really travels fast!

KENICKIE. Hey, listen, why didn't you tell me?

RIZZO. Don't worry about it, Kenickie. You don't even know who the guy is.

KENICKIE. Huh? Thanks a lot, kid.

(He walks away, hurt, leaves the party. The group urges him to stay. RIZZO, upset, sits looking after him.)

SONNY. *(coming over to RIZZO)* Hey, Rizz, how's tricks? Look, if you ever need somebody to talk to...

RIZZO. All of a sudden you think you can get a little. Get lost, Sonny.

DOODY. Tough luck, Rizzo.

ROGER. Listen, Rizz, I'll help you out with some money if you need it.

RIZZO. Forget it, I don't want any handouts.

FRENCHY. It ain't so bad, Rizz – you get to stay home from school.

JAN. Hey, you want to stay over tonight, Rizz?

RIZZO. Hey, why don't you guys just flake off and leave me alone?

(There is an awkward silence.)

JAN. It's getting late, anyway – I guess it might be better if everybody went home. C'mon, let's go!

(JAN pushes SONNY. DOODY and FRENCHY exit.)

MARTY. Hey, French...wait up!

(MARTY gets her purse, which is near RIZZO, avoiding eye contact. RIZZO glares viciously at her.)

ROGER. See ya, Rizz. *(ROGER looks at her a moment and exits.)*

SONNY. *(to JAN)* Tell her I didn't mean anything, will ya.

(He exits. RIZZO begins to clean up.)

JAN. Just leave that stuff, Rizzo. I'll get it.

RIZZO. Look, it's no bother. I don't mind.

(JAN exits. SANDY collects her record player and purse.)

SANDY. I'm sorry to hear you're in trouble, Rizzo.

RIZZO. Bull! What are you gonna do – give me a whole sermon about it?

SANDY. No. But doesn't it bother you that you're pregnant?

RIZZO. Look, that's my business. It's nobody else's problem.

SANDY. Do you really believe that? Didn't you see Kenickie's face when he left here?

(RIZZO turns away.)

It's Kenickie, isn't it? *(awkward pause)* Well, I guess I've said too much already. Good luck, Rizzo.

(She starts to leave. RIZZO turns and glares at her.)

RIZZO. Just a minute, Miss Goody-Goody! Who do you think you are? Handing me all this sympathy crap! Since you know all the answers, how come I didn't see Zuko here tonight? You just listen to me, Miss Sandra Dee…

(sings)

[MUSIC NO. 17: THERE ARE WORSE THINGS I COUL DO]

THERE ARE WORSE THINGS I COULD DO
THAN GO WITH A BOY OR TWO
EVEN THOUGH THE NEIGHBORHOOD
THINKS I'M TRASHY AND NO GOOD
I SUPPOSE IT COULD BE TRUE
BUT THERE'S WORSE THINGS I COULD DO.

I COULD FLIRT WITH ALL THE GUYS
SMILE AT THEM AND BAT MY EYES
PRESS AGAINST THEM WHEN WE DANCE
MAKE THEM THINK THEY STAND A CHANCE
THEN REFUSE TO SEE IT THROUGH
THAT'S A THING I'D NEVER DO.

I COULD STAY HOME EVERY NIGHT
WAIT AROUND FOR MISTER RIGHT
TAKE COLD SHOWERS EVERY DAY
AND THROW MY LIFE AWAY
FOR A DREAM THAT WON'T COME TRUE.

I COULD HURT SOMEONE LIKE ME
OUT OF SPITE OR JEALOUSY
I DON'T STEAL AND I DON'T LIE
BUT I CAN FEEL AND I CAN CRY
A FACT I'LL BET YOU NEVER KNEW
BUT TO CRY IN FRONT OF YOU
THAT'S THE WORST THING I COULD DO.

(Lights fade out on **RIZZO** as **SANDY** exits, crying carrying her record player, going into her bedroom. **SANDY** sits down on her bed, dejectedly. She sings a reprise)

[MUSIC NO. 18: LOOK AT ME, I'M SANDRA DEE]

SANDY.

> LOOK AT ME, THERE HAS TO BE
> SOMETHING MORE THAN WHAT THEY SEE
> WHOLESOME AND PURE, ALSO SCARED AND UNSURE
> A POOR MAN'S SANDRA DEE
>
> WHEN THEY CRITICIZE AND MAKE FUN OF ME
> CAN'T THEY SEE THE TEARS IN MY SMILE?
> DON'T THEY REALIZE THERE'S JUST ONE OF ME
> AND IT HAS TO LAST ME A WHILE.
>
> *(She picks up the phone and dials.)* Hello, Frenchy? Can
> you come over for a while? And bring your make-up
> case. *(She hangs up.)*
>
> SANDY, YOU MUST START ANEW
> DON'T YOU KNOW WHAT YOU MUST DO?
> HOLD YOUR HEAD HIGH
> TAKE A DEEP BREATH AND CRY
> GOODBYE
> TO SANDRA DEE.
>
> *(On last line of song she reaches for Kleenex and stuffs
> them into her bra. Lights fade.)*

**[MUSIC NO. 18A: SCENE CHANGE OUT OF
SANDRA DEE REPRISE]**

Scene Five

(Scene: Lights come up inside of the Burger Palace. **ROGER, DOODY, KENICKIE** *and* **SONNY** *are sitting at counter.)*

ROGER. Hey, you guys wanta come over to my house to watch the Mickey Mouse Club?

*(***PATTY*** *enters in cheerleader costume, dragging pom poms dispiritedly.)*

Do a split, give a yell, shake a tit for old Rydell. *(Optional line: Hey, whattaya say, Mary Hart-line?)*

*(***PATTY*** *ignores them.)*

SONNY. *(loudly)* She ain't talkin'.

DOODY. Maybe she had a fight with Danny.

KENICKIE. Hey, pom-poms! Why don't ya make me a track star too?

SONNY. Nah, get *me* out on that field. I'm a better broad-jumper than Zuko.

(The guys laugh.)

PATTY. *(turning on them)* You're disgusting, all of you! You can *have* your Danny Zuko, you worthless bums.

ROGER. Nice talk!

DOODY. Whatsa matter? Don't you like Danny anymore?

PATTY. As if you didn't know...he quit the track team!

ALL THE GUYS. Huh?

PATTY. I just found out. The other day the coach asked Danny, perfectly nicely, to get a hair cut. Danny made a shamefully crass gesture and walked off the field.

ROGER. What's a shamefully crass gesture?

SONNY. He gave him "the finger!"

(Guys crack up.)

ROGER. What a neat!

PATTY. Not only that, before he left the locker room, he…
he…smeared Ben-Gay in the team captain's athletic
supporter.

(The guys double up. **DANNY** *enters. The guys
immediately crowd around him.)*

DANNY. Hey, you guys!

KENICKIE. Hey, Zuko!

SONNY. Whattaya say, Zuke? Where ya been?

DOODY. Hi, Danny.

*(***DANNY*** stands open-mouthed, bewildered by all the
sudden attention.* **PATTY** *looks on disapprovingly.)*

DANNY. I guess you got the word, huh?

ROGER. Hey, come on, we were just goin' over to my house
to watch Mickey Mouse Club.

DANNY. *(enthusiastically)* Yeah?

PATTY. Danny! I want to talk to you.

*(***DANNY*** motions to guys to be cool for a second as he
crosses to* **PATTY.***)*

DANNY. Ease off, Patty!

PATTY. *(dagger eyes)* It's very *important,* Danny!

(Guys all crowd around **DANNY** *again.)*

SONNY. Aahh, come on! Zuko! It'll be neat. Annette's
startin' to get big knockers!

DANNY. *(smiles)* Solid! Later, Patty.

(Guys start to leave. **MARTY, FRENCHY, RIZZO** *and* **JAN**
*in Pink Ladies jackets enter silently, gesturing the guys
to "be cool" as they take up defiant positions.* **SANDY**
*enters, now a Greaser's "Dream Girl." A wild new hair
style, black leather motorcycle jacket with silver studs on
the back that spell "BIG D" skin tight slacks, gold hoop
earrings. Yet, she actually looks prettier and more alive
than she ever has. She is chewing gum and smoking a
cigarette. She slouches casually and French inhales.)*

RIZZO. *(aside, to* **SANDY***)* Remember, play it cool.

(**DANNY** *turns and sees* **SANDY**.)

DANNY. Hey, Sandy! Wow, what a total! Wick-ed!

SANDY. *(tough and cool)* What's it to ya', Zuko?

DANNY. Hey, we was just goin' to check out "The Mouse-keteers." How would you like to come along?

PATTY. Danny, what's gotten into you? You couldn't possibly be interested in that…that floozy.

(**SANDY** *looks to* **RIZZO** *for her next move. Then she strolls over to* **PATTY**, *studies her calmly, and punches her in the eye.* **PATTY** *falls.*)

RIZZO, FRENCHY, MARTY, JAN. YAA-AAY!

PATTY. Oh, my God, I'm going to have a black eye! (**PATTY** *bawls.*)

FRENCHY. *(opening purse)* Don't sweat it. I'll fix it up. I just got a job demonstrating this new miracle make-up at Wool-worth's.

DANNY. Hey, Sandy, you're somethin' else!

SANDY. Oh, so ya noticed, huh?

(She looks him calmly in the eye and walks coolly over to microphone, picks it up, walks back to **DANNY** *and then, making classic gesture with right hand striking left inner elbow; her left forearm swings up with mike in hand. Better known as an "up yours" gesture.)*

Tell me about it, stud!

[MUSIC NO. 19: ALL CHOKED UP]

DANNY. *(Sings.* **BURGER PALACE BOYS** *join in, doing background.)*
WELL, I FEEL SO STRANGE, WELL, UPON MY WORD
NOW MY BRAIN IS REELING AND MY EYESIGHT'S BLURRED
WELL, I TREMBLE A LOT
I'M NERVOUS AND I'M HOT
UH HUH! I'M ALL CHOKED UP

WELL, THERE'S A FIRE ALARM WAILIN' IN MY HEAD

AND MY CIRCULATION CRIES CONDITION RED
I'M IN A COLD SWEAT
MY T-SHIRT'S ALL WET
UH HUH! I'M ALL CHOKED UP

OH, BABY, BABY, BABY
TAKE MY HEART BEFORE IT BREAKS
MY KNEES ARE WEAK, MY BACKBONE QUAKES
MY HANDS ARE COLDER THAN ICE
MY THROAT IS LOCKED IN A VISE
COME ON CHANGE MY PAIN TO PARADISE

WELL, THERE'S A FEVER HEAT RUNNIN' THROUGH MY SKIN
DON'T YOU HEAR ME KNOCKIN', WON'T YOU LET ME IN
YOU KNOW I'M YOUR FOOL
SO DON'TCHA BE CRUEL
UH HUH! I'M ALL CHOKED UP!

GIRLS.

NOW. LISTEN HERE

SANDY.

SO YOU'RE SPINNIN' 'ROUND IN A DIZZY SPELL
IT'S A SITUATION I KNOW PRETTY WELL
WELL. I'VE BEEN THERE TOO
SO I FEEL FOR YOU
UH HUH! I'M ALL CHOKED UP

GIRLS.

AND FURTHERMORE

SANDY.

SO YOU'RE DOWN AND OUT, YOU'RE AGAINST A WALL
AND YOU SAY THAT I'M THE ONE THAT DID IT ALL
WELL, I'M SURE YOU'RE SINCERE
IT GETS ME RIGHT HERE
UH HUH! I'M ALL CHOKED UP
OH, BABY, TAKE IT SLOW AND DON'T COMPLAIN
MY POOR HEART JUST CAN'T STAND THE STRAIN
I CAN CURE YOUR DISEASE
C'MON AND SAY PRETTY PLEASE
TAKE YOUR MEDICINE DOWN ON YOUR KNEES!

DANNY & GUYS.

> GOT A FEVER, A HUNDRED FOUR FAHRENHEIT
> NEED YOUR LOVIN', CAN I COME OVER TONIGHT
> FEELIN' LOWDOWN, MY EQUILIBRIUM'S SHOT
> GIMME, GIMME, THAT TRANQUILIZER YOU'VE GOT

DANNY.

> OH, BABY, TAKE MY RING 'CAUSE YOU'RE MY MATCH

SANDY.

> WELL, I STILL THINK THERE'S STRINGS ATTACHED

DANNY.

> YOU'RE WRITIN' MY EPITAPH

SANDY.

> WELL THAT'S JUST TOUGH AND A HALF

DANNY.

> YOU'RE GONNA MAKE ME DIE!

SANDY.

> DON'T MAKE ME LAUGH!

DANNY & SANDY.

> WELL, I'LL FORGIVE WHAT YOU PUT ME THROUGH
> 'CAUSE I DO BELIEVE YOU REALLY LOVE ME TOO
> I LOOK IN YOUR EYES
> THE SUFFERIN' DIES
> UH HUH! I'M ALL CHOKED UP

ALL.

> HEY, HEY, HEY, YEAH
> I'M ALL CHOKED UP
> HEY, HEY HEY, YEAH

DANNY & SANDY.	**OTHERS.** *(Background.)*
I'M ALL CHOKED UP	HUM SHOO BEE DOO WOP
	HUM SHOO BEE DOO WOP
	HUM SHOO BEE DOO WOP

ALL.

> OW!

[MUSIC NO. 19A: CROSS OVER]

DANNY. Hey, I still got my ring! I guess you're still kinda mad at me, huh? *(He holds out his ring.)*

GIRLS.

ALWAYS BE TOGETHER.

BOYS.

CHANG CHANG CHANGITY CHANG SHOO BOP
CHANG CHANG CHANGITY CHANG SHOO BOP

GIRLS.

ALWAYS BE TOGETHER.

BOYS.

CHANG CHANG CHANGITY CHANG SHOO BOP
CHANG CHANG CHANGITY CHANG SHOO BOP

(The kids all have their arms around each other as they sing a one verse reprise of "We Go Together" and then go off dancing and singing.)

(curtain)

PROPERTY PLOT

PRESETS: (*onstage*)

    Downstage center cafeteria table covered with white table cloth
        (pennants and sign facing downstage)

    Rostrum on top of table with three green yearbooks on either side
    small business card left of Rostrum

    long green bench upstage of table with mike clips facing upstage

    Upstage left corner of stage right steps:

    1 spiral notebook

    1 textbook

    1 comic book

    1 bottle of coke

    2 slices of bread (to look like a sandwich) in cut-rite wax paper bag
        – place in brown paper bag

    Downstage right corner of stage right steps: (*on lowest step*)

    1 brown paper bag with orange

    water pistol

    1 binder

    1 textbook

    two cafeteria chairs on stage side of stage left tab

Sandy's Bed (on bed): On upper deck

    1 spread

    1 pillow

    1 throw pillow

    1 box kleenex

    6 stuffed animals (at head board)

    1 microphone (practical) – tucked under pillow

On End Table:

    1 lamp

    1 radio

Top Shelf:

    1 telephone

Bottom Shelf:

    2 stuffed animals

PRESETS: (*off right*)

For Act One, Scene 1 (Alma Mater and Parody): guitar

For Act One, Scene 2 (Cafeteria):

    brown paper bag with Pink "Hostess Snowball"

    binder

    textbook

    "Hot Rod" magazine

For Act One, Scene 3 (Magic Changes):

    textbook

    guitar chord book (Ronnie Dell)

For Act One, Scene 5 (Hub Cap):

    4 hub caps

1 *pair* of Red Foam Dice on red string
qt. beer bottle
tire iron
Car ("Greased Lightning") – containing:
Front-
>   box of Saran Wrap
>   panties
Back-
>   garter belt
>   bra
police siren and air horn
For Act One, Scene 6 (Baton):
four 2 inch strips of Johnson & Johnson white adhesive tape
For Act One, Scene 7 (Park):
Picnic Table
On Top:
>   6 pack coke (not practical)
>   6 beer cans (2 with drinkable water marked with tape)
>   3 hamburger rolls in wax paper bags
>   church key
>   qt. beer bottle
For Act Two, Scene 2 (track and rumble):
magazine (Hair-Do)
pack of Luckies
track relay baton
automobile antenna
For Act Two, Scene 4 (Basement):
Bar Unit with two stools on top:
>   bowl of Potato Chips
>   small bag of Popcorn
>   6 beer cans (2 with drinkable water – marked with tape)
>   6 pack of coke (not practical)
>   "View-Master" with slide
>   45 R.P.M. Turntable with records (4)
Sofa:
On top –
>   large throw pillow
>   guitar
>   canvas butterfly chair
PRESETS: (*off left*)
>   *For Act One, Scene 1 (Alma Mater and Parody):* black purse (Patty)
>   switchblade knife
>   *For Act One, Scene 2 (Cafeteria):*
>   *On Prop Table: 5 Tray Set Ups*
>   1. *Marty:*
>>   cafeteria tray
>>   knife, fork and spoon

large plate (rice pudding)
large bowl (fruit salad)
small bowl (rice pudding)
plastic "Glass" (interior painted purple – Grape)

Note: Attach Marty's plastic "glasses" to tray with *Velcro* all
others – glue
napkin
bubble gum
black looseleaf binder
magazine
purse: containing "Vogue" – cigarettes – comb – and
glasses

2. *Jan:*
cafeteria tray
fork and spoon
large plate (rice pudding)
2 small bowls (rice pudding and fruit salad)
large bowl (fruit salad)
plastic "glass" (interior – white – milk)
banana
napkin
bubble gum
looseleaf binder
textbook
purse: containing datebook

3. *Sandy:*
cafeteria tray
knife and fork
large plate
small bowl (rice pudding)
plastic glass (interior – white)
napkin
looseleaf binder
term paper binder
textbook
purse: containing comb

4. *Frenchy:*
cafeteria tray
fork and spoon
large plate (fruit salad)
plastic "Glass" (interior-Purple)
napkin
bubble gum
large black looseleaf binder
2 magazines (movie star)
green purse: containing

makeup stick

emory board

    5. *Rizzo:*

        cafeteria tray

        large plate (fruit salad)

        knife, fork and spoon

        large bowl (fruit salad)

        small bowl (fruit salad)

        plastic "Glass" (interior – Purple)

        bubble gum

        napkin

        black purse with long arm strap

pack of small colored cards (6)

class schedule

purse

black binder

brown paper bag: 2 apples

For Act One, Scene 3 (Magic Changes):

2 green pom-poms

book

eraser

For Act One, Scene 4 (Pajama Party):

Bed with end table on headboard:

    Black "Pinklady" Jacket

    "Virgin Pin" – (pinned on jacket)

On end table:

Top:

    make-up mirror (soaped) on stand

    ashtray

    book of matches

In Drawer:

    red nail polish

    matches

On Shelf Below:

    stuffed animal

    hat box

    kleenex

    2 books

Vanity Table In Drawer:

    wallet containing long series of pictures, marked picture removable

    wallet surrounded by 3 rubber bands

On Top Of Table:

    Ashtray: containing "Hit Parade" cigarettes; 4 loose cigarettes

    book of matches

    magazine (open)

Underneath Table:

> foot stool

Chair:

> *On Top of:*
>
> > ½ gallon "Italian Swiss Colony" bottle partially filled with "wine" in Brown paper bag

Blanket:

> *On Top of:*
>
> > portable radio
> >
> > "Twinkies"
> >
> > comic book

For Act One, Scene 6 (Baton):

2 batons

For Act One, Scene 7 (Park):

2 45-degree angle park benches, one stacked upside down on top of the other battered trash can blanket

3 magazines

3 qt. beer bottles

beer can

2 bags of leaves

For Act Two, Scene 1 (Hop):

red "Johnny Casino" guitar (not practical)

pint whiskey bottle filled with water

For Act Two, Scene 2 (Track, B. S. D., Rumble):

lead

pipe chain

baseball bat

zip gun (covered with rubber band)

white rolled "Diploma" (tied with red ribbon)

For Act Two, Scene 3 (Drive-In):

Car in front seat:

> 1 qt. beer bottle (in brown paper bag)
>
> purse (Sandy)

For Act Two, Scene 5 (Burger):

Burger Booth Unit

Burger Counter and Stool Unit

on top of:

> menu

Inside:

> bucket containing coke bottle with coke

Act Two – Presets on Stage:

Hop Table – upstage center between columns on top of:

    green table cloth with "coconuts" and green crepe streamers

    punch bowl

    ladle

    8 cups

    card of tacks

    pink crepe streamer

Long Green Bench – downstage left on marks

Tray of Prizes – upper deck D. L. corner of bedroom platform

    2 record albums ("Hits From The House of Wax")

    2 – 3 x 5 cards (movie passes)

    1 – 2 x 3 card (gift certificate)

    2 trophies

STAGE LEFT RUNNING PLOT:

ACT ONE

During Act One, Scene 1 (Parody):
> *Catch :*
>> black purse from girl, "Patty"
>> SET in first section of prop table

During Act One, Scene 2 (Cafeteria):
> fold table cloth and store
> store green yearbooks

During Act One, Scene 3 (Magic Changes):
> clear cafeteria table
> place dishes in strainer
> store table u. s.
> wipe off trays and *re-set* on prop table

During Act One, Scene 4 (Pajama Party):
> *Set: On Prop Table*
>> 3 quart beer bottles
>> 1 beer can
>> 1 blanket
>> 2 magazines
>> 1 black handbag ("Rizzo")

During Act One, Scene 5 (Hubcap):
> *Catch:*
>> bed
>> dresser
>> chair
>> clear cigarettes, matches, etc., from dresser place in drawer
>> replace picture in wallet
> *Set:*
>> green table cloth
>> punch bowl with ladle and paper cups (two stacks of four each)
>> roll of crepe streamers, pack of thumbtacks on dresser
>> "Virgin Pin" on "Pink Lady" jacket on bed

Durning Act One, Scene 6 (Baton):
> *Car comes off:*
>> clear and take s.r. saran wrap, bra, panties, garterbelt, hubcaps and dice
> *Preset: In Front Seat*
>> 1 qt. beer bottle in brown paper bag
>> "Sandy's" purse
>> park benches to go on.

During Intermission:
> *Strike:*

3 qt. beer bottles, 1 beer can, trash can, books from lockers, pom-poms from Upper Deck

Stage Left Running Plot:

    Preset for Act Two:

        (On Upper Deck), prizes on tray downstage left corner of bedroom platform

        2 trophies

        2 record albums

        2 – 5 x 3 cards

        1 – 3 x 2 card

        long green bench downstage left on marks

        hop table upstage center between columns

        book in fourth locker from center on bottom

        coke bottle (with coke) in bucket in burger counter unit

        books and dishes on trays (Prop Table)

During Act Two, Scene 2 (Track):

    take red guitar from actor on upper deck ("Casino") hang on prop shelf take hip table from actresses ("Lynch and Patty") clear and

    store cloth etc. Store dresser with other bedroom pieces. Take green bench from actor ("Eugene") and store u. s.

During Act Two, Scene 3 (Drive-in):

    Store:

        lead pipe and chain, baseball bat, zipgun

        take aerial s. R.

During Act Two, Scene 4 (Basement):

    Strike:

        beer bottle from car and store

    Set: Burger Units In Position to go on

        1. Booth

        2. Counter

During Act Two, Scene 5 (Burger):

    Catch:

        Burger counter unit from actor ("Eugene") and store

Stage Right Running Plot – Act One:

During Act One, Scene 2: (Cafeteria):

    take green yearbooks from lady ("Lynch")

    take scrim leg from man ("Kenickie") and store u. s.

During Act One, Scene 5 (Hubcap):

    as car goes on, move picnic table down to same preset position car was in

During Intermission:

    clear mikes from picnic table and strike picnic table

PRESET:

    On Bar Unit with two stools:

        6 pack of coke

6 beer cans (2 with drinkable water – marked with tape)

1 small bag of popcorn

1 bowl of potato chips set bar unit in position originally used by car downstage of bar

Set sofa with large throw pillow and wire frame butterfly chair

During Act Two, Scene 5 (Burger):

    Catch:

        bar unit

        sofa

        wire framed butterfly chair with large throw pillow and store

    Strike:

        two green "pom-poms"

    Catch:

        "Burger" booth unit and store

Running Plot – Act One:

During Act One, Scene 2 (Cafeteria):

    take green yearbooks from stage right and tablecloth from upstage center to stage left

    fold cloth and store

    store yearbooks

During Act One, Scene 3 (Magic Changes): clear cafeteria table

    Set:

        trays and books on prop table

During Act One, Scene 4 (Pajama Party):

    store cafeteria chairs upstage

During Act One, Scene 5 (Greased Lightning):

    Catch:

        bed and chair

    Store:

        blanket with comic wrapped in it

During Act One, Scene 6 (Baton):

    Position park benches to go on wash dishes

During Intermission:

    Strike:

        blanket stage left

        magazines stage left

        park benches stage left

    take:

        leaf bag from stage right to stage left and store

        store beer cans and bottle stage left

Running Plot – Act Two:

During Act Two, Scene 2 (Track):

    Take:

        prizes from right and store stage left

COSTUME PLOT

DANNY ZUKO:

Act One, Scene 2:

Black stretch pants with pink stitching on sides, white T-Shirt, leather jacket, belt, white socks, blue suede shoes, medal and chain, switch blade.

Act One, Scene 3:

Same as in Act One, Scene 2.

Act One, Scene 5:

Same as Act One, Scene Two minus the black leather jacket.

Act One, Scene 6:

Add: Purple W/ white trim short sleeve shirt (unbuttoned;.

Act One, Scene 7:

Same as Act One, Act 2.

Act Two, Scene 1:

Black stretch slacks, red socks, blue suede shoes, black tricot see thru shirt, red sport jacket with silver lining.

Act Two, Scene 2:

White track suit (Green trim shorts and tank top), white socks, white basketball sneakers, neck chain and medal.

Act Two, Scene 3:

Purple pull-over shirt with grey piping, black stretch slacks, white socks, blue suede shoes, neck chain and medal.

Act Two, Scene 5:

Black stretch slacks, black sleeveless T-shirt, black leather jacket, neck chain and medal, white socks, blue suede shoes

SANDY DUMBROWSKI:

Act One, Scene 2:

Pink and white striped shirt blouse, grey felt circle skirt with pink poodle trim, cinch belt (Clear plastic if possible), white socks, brown loafers, blue hair ribbon.

Act One, Scene 4:

Small floral print on Baby blue background floor length bathrobe, fluffy fur slippers, blue ribbon.

Act One, Scene 6:

Gym suit (should be "Rydell Green" with name lettered on in white), white socks, white sneakers, blue hair ribbon, white adhesive tape under left ear lobe.

Act One, Scene 7:

Same as Act One, Scene 2. Change to white cinch belt, black capezios, white ribbon.

Act Two, Scene 1:

Same as Act One, Scene 4.

Act Two, Scene 2:

White slip, white slippers, white on white striped plastic shower curtain cape, white hair net, white roller head piece.

Act Two, Scene 3:

Pale blue straight skirt, white ruffled nylon blouse, hair ribbon, blue heels.

Act Two, Scene 4:

Blue and grey plaid tight skirt, white "angora" bead trimmed sweater, black capezios, hair ribbon.

Act Two, Scene 5:

Chartreuse-y green pedal pushers, black leotard top, black cinch belt, black leather jacket, black capezios, flashy earrings (Jacket is studded on back to say "Big D"

.

MISS LYNCH:

Act One, Scene 1:

Black full slip, black back-ground white flower print dress, black pumps, pearl necklace.

Act One, Scene 2:

Same as Act One, Scene 1.

Act Two, Scene 1:

Same as Act One, Scene 1. Add: Flower corsage, pearl necklace.
Curtain:

Same as Act One, Scene 1.

PATTY SIMCOX:

Act One, Scene 1:

Black skirt, grey jacket, black and white scarf, black shoes, black shoulder purse, gold earrings.

Act One, Scene 2:

Green and brown pleated skirt (Cheerleader skirt), Cheerleader sweater, green and brown hair ribbon, white socks, white sneakers, "Vote Patty" cardboard campaign pin on sweater.

Act One, Scene 6:

Same as in Act One, Scene 2.

Act Two, Scene 1:

Pink prom dress with crinolines, pink heels, wrist corsage.

Act Two, Scene 2:

White slip, white slippers, white on white striped plastic shower curtain cape, white hair net, white roller head piece,

Act Two, Scene 5:

Same as Act One, Scene 2.

EUGENE FLORCZYK:

Scene One, Scene 1:

Grey suit, white shirt, red tie, black shoes.

Act One, Scene 7:

Camel Boy scout bermudas, white shirt, green sweater, yellow and brown argyle socks, brown loafers.

Act Two, Scene 1:

White formal shirt, cuff links and studs, Black 50's Tuxedo, white buck shoes, grey and black argyle socks, yellow plaid bow tie and cumberbund. *Curtain:*

Same as Act One, Scene 1.

JAN:

Act One, Scene 2:

Plaid pleated skirt, red sweater with white angora trim at top, (short sleeved) yellow scarf, white socks, black capezios.

Act One, Scene 3:

Same as in Act One, Scene 2. Act One, Scene 4:

Bright yellow print pajama top (shortie) and panties, white socks.

Act One, and Scene 7:

Red sweater, flower print pedal pushers, yellow scarf, Pink Lady Jacket, white socks, black capezios.

Act Two, Scene 1:

Blue brocade Prom dress, white capezios, rhinestone head band, white crinoline.

Act Two, Scene 2:

White slip, white slippers, white on white striped plastic shower curtain cape, white hair net, white roller head piece.

Act Two, Scene 4:

Same as Act One, Scene 2.

Act Two, Scene 5:

Flower print pedal pushers, red sweater, yellow scarf on head, white socks, black capezios, Pink Lady Jacket.

MARTY:

Act One, Scene 2:

Black straight skirt, sky blue cardigan sweater, pink and blue scarf, Pink Lady jacket, white socks, black capezios, flashy earrings.

Act One, Scene 3:

Same as in Act One, Scene 2.

Act One, Scene 4:

Pink pajama top and panties, gold short heel slippers, pink head band, gold earrings, short red Japanese Kimono.

Act One, Scene 7:

Black skirt, sky blue sweater, black capezios, blue and white scarf, blue hair hand, white letter sweater with "H.C."

Act Two, Scene 1:

Gold beaded sweater, tight gold skirt, gold heels, big earrings, head band.

Act Two, Scene 2:

White slip, white slippers, white on white striped plastic shower curtain cape, white hair net, white roller head piece.

Act Two, Scene 4:

Black skirt, sky blue sweater, blue and white scarf, purple head band, black capezios, Pink Lady Jacket worn around waist.

Act Two, Scene 5:

Same as Act One, Scene 2.

BETTY RIZZO:

Act One, Scene 2:

Tight blue straight skirt, turquoise blue fuzzy (Angora type) long sleeve sweater, Pink Lady Jacket, red capezios, anklets (Underdress: Pajama bottoms red and white striped pull-over jersey.

Act One, Scene 3:

Same as Act One, Scene 2.

Act One, Scene 4:

Blue or green pajama top and panties, red capezios (Under-dress: red and white striped top) (Preset: White pedal pushers).

Act One, Scene 5:

White pedal pushers, red and white striped top, black cinch belt, red Capezios.

Act One, Scene 7:

Add: Pink Lady Jacket.

Act Two, Scene 1:

Black Prom dress, black heels.

Act Two, Scene 2:

White slip, white slippers, white on white striped plastic shower curtain cape, white hair net, white roller head piece.

Act Two, Scene 4:

White pedal pushers, turquoise fuzzy sweater, red capezios.

Act Two, Scene 5:

White pedal pushers, turquoise fuzzy sweater, red capezios, Pink Lady Jacket.

DOODY:

Act One, Scene 2:

Blue jeans, white T-shirt, red plaid flannel shirt, white socks, black belt, brown penny loafers.

Act One, Scene 3:

Same as in Act One, Scene 2.

Act One, Scene 5:

Blue jeans, white T-shirt with V-neck, white socks, brown loafers.

Act One, Scene 7:

Same as Act One, Scene 2.

Act Two, Scene 1:

Black cuff slacks, pink and black shirt, white sport coat, white socks, brown loafers.

Act Two, Scene 2:

Blue jeans, red, blue and white pull-over, windbreaker-type shirt, white socks, loafers.

Act Two, Scene 4:

Same as Act One, Scene 2.

Act Two, Scene 5:

Same as Act One, Scene 2.

ROGER:

Act One, Scene 2:

Grey slacks with pink stitching on sides, white T-shirt, burgundy windbreaker, white socks, engineer boots.

Act One, Scene 3:

Same as in Act One, Scene 2.

Act One, Scene 5:

Grey pants, white T-shirt, white socks, engineer boots.

Act One, Scene 7:

Add: Hawaiian flowered shirt (unbuttoned), brown loafers.

Act Two, Scene 1:

Grey slacks, yellow plaid shirt, pink sport jacket, white socks, brown loafers.

Act Two, Scene 2:

Blue jeans with special velcro, white T-shirt, burgundy wind-breaker, white socks, brown loafers.

Act Two, Scene 4:

Grey slacks, yellow plaid shirt, white socks, brown loafers.

Act Two, Scene 5:

Same as Act One, Scene 2.

KENICKIE:

Act One, Scene 2:

Blue jeans, black T-shirt, silver belt, black leather jacket.

Act One, Scene 3:

Same as in Act One, Scene 2.

Act One, Scene 5:

Same as Act One, Scene Two.

Act One, Scene 7:

Same as in Act One, Scene 2.

Act Two, Scene 1:

Grey slacks, black embroidered cowboy shirt, bola tie, madras sport jacket, black socks, boots, red bandana hankerchief in right pants pocket.

Act Two, Scene 2:

Grey slacks, black T-shirt, grey belt, black leather jacket, black socks, boots.

Act Two, Scene 4:

Blue jeans, black cowboy shirt, black socks, boots.

Act Two, Scene 5:

Same as in Act One, Scene 2.

SONNY LATIERRI:

Act One, Scene 2:

Black slacks, white T-shirt, black shirt, chain and medal, tan leather jacket, white socks, black pointed shoes, small black brim hat, dark glasses, black belt.

Act One, Scene 3:

Same as in Act 1, Scene 2.

Act One, Scene 5:

Black pants, white socks, black pointed shoes, black belt, white
tank top undershirt, black brim hat.

Act One, Scene 7:

Same as Act One, Scene 5 minus black hat. Add: Tan leather
jacket.

Act Two, Scene 1:

Black slacks, black shirt, white tie, shiny green sport coat, white
socks, black pointed shoes.

Act Two, Scene 2:

Same as Act One, Scene 2 minus dark glasses.

Act Two, Scene 4:

Same as Act One, Scene 2 minus dark glasses, black hat and tan
leather jacket.

Act Two, Scene 5:

Same as Act One, Scene 2 minus hat and dark glasses.

FRENCHY:

Act One, Scene 2:

Grey tweed straight skirt with godets, hot pink sweater, pink scarf,
Pink Lady Jacket, white socks, black capezios, flashy earrings.

Act One, Scene 3:

Same as in Act One, Scene 2.

Act One, Scene 4:

Lavender shorty pajamas top and panties, white socks.

Act One, Scene 7:

Same as Act One, Scene 2.

Act Two, Scene 1:

Nylon green blouse, black velvet diagonally striped skirt, green
high heels (pointy toed spikes), flashy earrings.

Act Two, Scene 2:

Same as in Act One, Scene 2.

Act Two, Scene 4:

Same as in Act One, Scene 2 minus Pink Lady jacket.

Act Two, Scene 5:

Same as in Act One, Scene 2.

VINCE FONTAINE:

Act Two, Scene 1:

Black tuxedo slacks, gold dress shirt, cuff links, studs, black
cummerbund, black bow tie, leopard tuxedo jacket, black
socks, black patent leather shoes.

Curtain:
Same as in Act Two, Scene 1.

JOHNNY CASINO:

Act Two, Scene 1:

Geranium pink slacks with dark pink stripes on side, pink ruffed formal shirt, large cuff links, red bow tie, pink plaid tuxedo jacket with red satin lapels, white socks, pink and red two-tone wing tipped shoes, red cummerbund.

CHA-CHA DEGREGORIO:

Act Two, Scene 1:

Yellow taffeta prom dress with crinolines, yellow tyette shoes, yellow hair ribbon, yellow and green poppet bead necklace.

Act Two, Scene2.:

White slip, white slippers, white on white striped plastic shower curtain cape, white hair net, white roller head piece. *Curtain:*

Same as Act 2, Scene 1.

TEEN ANGEL:

Act Two, Scene 2:

White sweater, white slacks, white socks, white bucks. *Curtain:*

Same as in Act Two, Scene 2.

COSTUMES: RUNNING ORDER

Act One, Scene 1: (Class of '59 Reunion)

MISS LYNCH:

Black full slip, black back-ground white flower print dress, black pumps, pearl necklace.

EUGENE:

Grey suit, white shirt, black-grey stripe tie, black shoes.

PATTY:

Black skirt, grey jacket, black and white scarf, black shoes, black shoulder purse, gold earrings.

Act One, Scene 2: (Parody – Cafeteria – School Steps)

DANNY:

Black stretch pants with pink stitching on sides, white T-shirt, leather jacket, belt, white socks, blue suede shoes, medal and chain, switch blade.

KENICKIE:

Blue jeans, black T-shirt, silver belt, black leather jacket, black socks, boots.

ROGER:

Grey slacks with pink stitching on sides, white T-shirt, burgundy windbreaker, white socks, engineer boots.

SONNY:

Black slacks, white T-shirt, black shirt, chain and medal, tan leather jacket, white socks, black pointed shoes, small black brim hat, dark glasses, black belt.

DOODY:

Blue jeans, white T-shirt, red plaid flannel shirt, white socks, black belt, brown penny loafers.

RIZZO:

Tight blue straight skirt, turquoise blue fuzzy (Angora-type) long sleeve sweater, Pink Lady Jacket, red capezios, anklet, (Under dress: Pajamas bottoms, red and white striped pull-over jersey).

FRENCHY:

Grey tweed straight skirt with godets, hot pink sweater, pink scarf, Pink Lady Jacket, white socks, black capezios, flashy earrings.

JAN:

Plaid pleated skirt, red sweater with white angora trim at top, short sleeved, yellow scarf, white socks, black capezios

MARTY:

Black straight skirt, sky blue cardigan sweater, pink and blue scarf, Pink Lady Jacket, pink hair band, earrings, black capezios, pink eye frames with rhinestones.

SANDY:

Pink and white striped shirt blouse, grey felt circle skirt with pink poodle trim, cinch belt (clear plastic if possible), white socks, brown loafers, blue hair ribbon.

PATTY:

Green and brown pleated cheerleader skirt, cheerleader sweater, green and brown hair ribbon, white socks, white sneakers, "VOTE PATTY" cardboard campaign pin on sweater.

MISS LYNCH:

Same as Act One, Scene 1.

Act One, Scene 3: (Magic Changes)

Same as in Act One, Scene 2.

Act One, Scene 4: (Pajama Party) All Pajamas are shorty

FRENCHY:

Lavender shorty pajamas top and panties, white socks.

JAN:

Bright yellow print pajama top and panties, white socks.

RIZZO:

Blue or green pajama top and panties, red capezios (Under-dress: Red and white striped top) (Preset: White pedal pushers).

MARTY:

Pink pajama top and panties, gold short heel slippers, pink head band, gold earrings, short red Japanese Kimono.

SANDY:

Small floral print on Baby blue background floor length bathrobe, fluffy fur slippers, blue ribbon.

Act One, Scene 5: (Greased Lightning)

DANNY: Same as Act One, Scene Two minus the black leather jacket.

SONNY:

Same as Act One, Scene 2 minus white T-shirt, dark glasses, black shirt, tan leather jacket. Add: Tank top undershirt.

DANNY:

Black stretch pants, white T-shirt, black belt, white socks, blue suede shoes, neck chain and medal.

SONNY:

Black pants, white socks, black pointed shoes, black belt, white tank top undershirt, black brim hat.

ROGER:

Grey pants, white T-shirt, white socks, engineer boots.

DOODY:

Blue jeans, white T-shirt with V-neck, white socks, brown loafers.

RIZZO:

White pedal pushers, red and white striped top, black cinch belt, red capezios.

KENICKIE:

Same as in Act One, Scene 2.

Act One, Scene 6: (Baton Scene)

SANDY:

Gym suit (should be "Rydell Green" with name lettered on in white), white socks, white sneakers, blue hair ribbon, white adhesive tape under left ear lobe.

PATTY:

Same as in Act One, Scene 2.

DANNY: Add: Purple with white trim short sleeve shirt (unbuttoned)

Act One, Scene 7: (Park Scene)

ROGER: Add: Hawaiian flowered shirt (unbuttoned), brown loafers.

JAN:

Red sweater, flower print pedal pushers, yellow scarf, Pink Lady Jacket, white socks, black capezios.

DANNY:

Same as Act One, Scene 2.

MARTY:

Black skirt, sky blue sweater, black capezios, blue and white scarf, blue hair band, white letter sweater with "H.C."

RIZZO: Add: Pink Lady Jacket

KENICKIE:

Same as Act One, Scene 2 and Act One, Scene 5.

EUGENE:

Camel Boy scout bermudas, white shirt, green sweater, yellow and brown argyle socks, brown loafers.

SANDY:

Same as Act One, Scene 2. Change to white cinch belt, black capezios, white hair ribbon.

DOODY:

Same as Act One, Scene 2.

FRENCHY:

Same as Act One, Scene 2.

SONNY:

Same as Act One, Scene 5 minus black hat, Add: Tan leather jacket.

Act Two, Scene 1: (Shakiri – Hand Jive Contest)

DANNY:

Black stretch slacks, red socks, blue suede shoes, black tricot see thru shirt, red sports jacket with silver lining.

RIZZO:

Black prom dress, black heels.

FRENCHY:

Nylon green blouse, black velvet diagonally striped skirt, green high heels (pointy toed spikes), flashy earrings.

JAN:

Blue brocade Prom dress, white capezios, rhinestone head band, white crinoline.

MARTY:

Gold beaded sweater, tight gold skirt, gold heels, big earrings, head band.

KENICKIE:

Grey slacks, black embroidered cowboy shirt, bola tie, madras sport jacket, black socks, boots, red bandana hankerchief in right pants pocket.

SONNY:

Black slacks, black shirt, white tie, shiny green sports coat, white socks, black pointed shoes.

ROGER:

Grey slacks, yellow plaid shirt, pink sport jacket, white socks, brown loafers.

DOODY:

Black cuff slacks, pink and black shirt, white sport coat, white socks, brown loafers.

EUGENE:

White formal shirt, cuff links and studs, Black 50's Tuxedo, white buck shoes, grey and black argyle socks, yellow plaid bow rings.

MISS LYNCH:

Same as Act One, Scene 1, Add: Flower corsage, pearl necklace.

PATTY:

Pink prom dress, pink heels, wrist corsage (Dress with crinolines).

JOHNNY CASINO:

Geranium pink slacks with dark pink stripes on side, pink ruffled formal shirt, large cuff links, red bow tie, pink plaid tuxedo jacket with red satin lapels, white socks, pink and red two-tone wing tipped shoes, red cummerbund.

VINCE FONTAINE:

Black tuxedo slacks, gold dress shirt, cuff links, studs, black cummerbund, black bow tie, leopard tuxedo jacket, black socks, black patent leather shoes.

CHA-CHA:

Yellow taffeta prom dress with crinolines, yellow tyette shoes, yellow hair ribbon, yellow and green poppet bead necklace.

SANDY:

Same as Act One, Scene 4.

Act Two, Scene 2: (Beauty School Dropout)

KENICKIE:

Grey slacks, black T-shirt, grey belt, black leather jacket, black socks, boots.

SONNY:

Same as Act One, Scene 2 minus dark glasses.

DOODY:

Blue jeans, red, blue and white pull-over windbreaker-type shirt, white socks, loafers.

FRENCHY:

Same as Act One, Scene 2.

GIRLS:

White slips, white slippers, white on white striped plastic shower curtain capes, white hair net, white roller head piece.

TEEN ANGEL:

White sweater, white slacks, white socks, white bucks.

DANNY:

White track suit (green trim shorts and tank top), white socks, white basketball sneakers, neck chain and medal.

ROGER:

Blue jeans with special velcro, white T-shirt, burgundy windbreaker, white socks, brown loafers.

Act Two, Scene 3: (Drive-in Movie)

DANNY:

Purple pull-over shirt with grey piping, black stretch slacks, white socks, blue suede shoes, neck chain and medal.

SANDY:

Pale blue straight skirt, white ruffled nylon blouse, hair ribbon, blue heels.

Act Two, Scene 4: (**JAN**'s *basement*)

SANDY:

Blue and grey plaid tight skirt, white "angora" bead-trimmed sweater, black capezios, hair ribbon.

RIZZO: White pedal pushers, turquoise fuzzy sweater, red capezios.

MARTY:

Black skirt, sky blue sweater, blue and white scarf, purple head band, black capezios, Pink Lady Jacket worn around waist.

FRENCHY:

Same as Act One, Scene 2 minus Pink Lady Jacket.

JAN:

Same as Act One, Scene 2.

KENICKIE:

Blue jeans, black cowboy shirt, black socks, boots.

ROGER:

Grey slacks, yellow plaid shirt, white socks, brown loafers.

SONNY:

Same as Act One, Scene 2 minus dark glasses, black hat and tan leather jacket.

Act Two, Scene 5: (*Burger Palace Interior*) **ROGER:**

Same as Act One, Scene 2.

SONNY: Same as Act One, Scene 2 minus hat and dark glasses.

KENICKIE:

Same as Act One, Scene 2*

DOODY:

Same as Act One, Scene 2.

PATTY:

Same as Act One, Scene 2.

DANNY:

Black stretch slack*, black sleeveless T-shirt, black leather jacket, neck chain and medal, white socks, blue suede shoes.

RIZZO:

White pedal pushers, turquoise fuzzy sweater, red capezios, Pink Lady Jacket.

JAN:

Flower print pedal pushers, red sweater, yellow scarf on head, white socks, black capezios, Pink Lady Jacket.

FRENCHY:

Same as Act One, Scene 2.

MARTY:

Same as Act One, Scene 2.

SANDY:

Chartreuse-y green pedal pushers, black leotard top, black cinch belt, black leather jacket, black capezios, flashy earrings. (Jacket is studded on back to say "BIG D"). *Curtain Calls:*

CHA-CHA:

Same as Act Two, Scene 1.

TEEN ANGEL:

Same as Act Two, Scene 2.

VINCE FONTAINE:

Same as Act Two, Scene 1.

MISS LYNCH:

Same as Act One, Scene 1.

EUGENE:

Same as Act One, Scene 1.

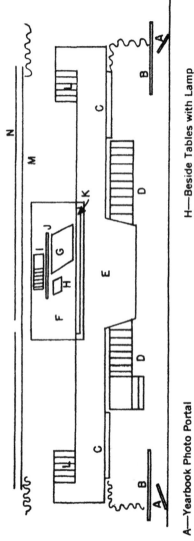

A—Yearbook Photo Portal
B—#1 Greaser Wings
C—#2 Greaser Wings
D—Moving School Stairs
E—Elevated Platform
F—Sandy's Bedroom (Elevated)
G—Sandy's Bed

H—Beside Tables with Lamp
I—Escape Stairs
J—Sandra Dee Blow-up Photo
K—James Dean Photo
L—Escape Stairs
M—Photo Collage Drop
N—Brick Wall Drop

FLOOR PLAN
"GREASE"

SANDY. Nah. The hell with it! *(They kiss and hug quickly.)*

ROGER. *(crossing to* **JAN***)* Hey, we just gonna stand around here all day? Let's get outta here!

DOODY. Yeah, we're missin' "Anything-Can-Happen" Day!

*(***FRENCHY*** *joins* **DOODY***.)*

DANNY. Yeah, let's cut! You comin', "Big D"?

SANDY. Solid! Hey, Patty, you wanna come?

PATTY. Oh. Well, thanks, but I wouldn't want to be in the way.

SANDY. Nah. It don't matter. Right?

DANNY. Hell no, c'mon, Patty!

*(***PATTY*** *crosses up to door near* **DANNY***.)*

SONNY. *(goes over to* **MARTY***)* Hey, Marty, did I tell ya I'm gettin' a new Impala?

MARTY. Ohh, would you paint my name on it?

*(***SONNY*** *nods "sure" and puts arm around her. They head for door area.)*

RIZZO. *(crossing to* **KENICKIE***)* Hey, Kenickie, can we stop at the drugstore? I think I'm getting my friend.

*(***KENICKIE*** *puts arm around her as all kids smile and cheer for* **RIZZO***.)*

FRENCHY. Gee, the whole crowd's together again. I could cry.

JAN. Gee, me too!

SANDY. Yeah. A wop-baba-lu-bop!

[MUSIC NO. 19A: CROSS OVER]

ENSEMBLE.
WE'RE FOR EACH OTHER
LIKE A WOP BOB-A-LU-MOP AND WOP BAM BOOM.
JUST LIKE MY BROTHER IS
SHAN-NA-NA-NA-NA-NA-NA YIPPITY DIP-DE-DOOM
CHANG CHANG CHANGITTY CHANG SHOO BOP,
WE'LL ALWAYS E TOGETHER, WHA OOH, YEAH.